"What should a man do were he to be sitting opposite the object of his desire?"

Bruno reached out and covered Katy's hand with his and then turned it over so that he could stroke her palm very softly with his thumb.

For a few seconds Katy was so startled that she literally froze. Then came a rush of heat that was so intense it made her head swim and her pulse race and sent funny, pleasurable little sensations racing to her breasts and between her legs. It made her feel weak and squirmy and…

She snatched her hand away, horribly confused.

Bruno felt a cold emptiness where her hand had lain in his and wondered, fleetingly, what the hell had just gone on there. A bit of nothing that had felt like a lot of something, though he couldn't for the life of him say what. He obviously had a load of pent-up sexual energy that needed rel

"Stop it!" Kly sharp. "It's

D1374298

*Getting to know him in the boardroom—
and the bedroom!*

A secret romance, a forbidden affair,
a thrilling attraction…

What happens when two people work together
and simply can't help falling in love—
no matter how hard they try to resist?

Find out in our ongoing series of stories
set in the world of work.

Coming in June:

Mistress by Agreement #2402
by
Helen Brooks

Available only from Harlequin Presents®

Cathy Williams

HIS VIRGIN SECRETARY

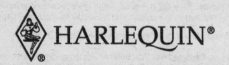

TORONTO • NEW YORK • LONDON
AMSTERDAM • PARIS • SYDNEY • HAMBURG
STOCKHOLM • ATHENS • TOKYO • MILAN • MADRID
PRAGUE • WARSAW • BUDAPEST • AUCKLAND

ISBN 0-373-12390-6

HIS VIRGIN SECRETARY

First North American Publication 2004.

Copyright © 2004 by Cathy Williams.

This edition published by arrangement with Harlequin Books S.A.

® and TM are trademarks of the publisher. Trademarks indicated with ® are registered in the United States Patent and Trademark Office, the Canadian Trade Marks Office and in other countries.

Visit us at www.eHarlequin.com

Printed in U.S.A.

CHAPTER ONE

BRUNO was coming, flying back from New York, and Katy knew that there was just no way that she was going to be able to do her usual and disappear the minute he arrived.

Bruno Giannella, put quite simply, terrified her. She had first met him eighteen months ago, when she had been subjected to an interview that had paid lip service to his opening words—that he just wanted to discover a bit about her, considering the role she would have in his godfather's life. Thereafter had followed the most gruelling hour and a half she had ever endured, which had left her in no doubt that the only way she could possibly get along with the man was to have as little to do with him as possible.

Since then, she had managed to turn evasion into an art form. His visits to his godfather were fleeting, infrequent and pre-planned. Bruno Giannella was not, she had long concluded, comfortable with spontaneity. Impulse did not feature highly in a life that seemed to have been programmed right down to the last minute. It was something for which she was eternally grateful because it gave her ample opportunity to coincide her departures from the house with exquisite timing, either just missing him or else seeing him while virtually on the hop.

Now, however, there was to be no such easy avoidance.

Joseph, his godfather, had been rushed to hospital with a suspected heart attack the afternoon before. It had all been a tremendous shock and as soon as things had quietened down somewhat she had telephoned his godson to tell him what had happened. It spoke volumes that she had had to call nearly a dozen numbers before she had eventually been put through to him in his New York office and when she finally had made contact, she'd been subjected to a thinly veiled implication that she had somehow taken her time getting in touch with him. No sooner had she stammered her way into her explanation about the difficulties she had had discovering his precise whereabouts, than he'd been briskly informing her that he would be on his way back to England immediately and that he would expect her to be at the house when he arrived the following day. The click of the telephone being hung up on her when she'd been virtually in mid-sentence had been an apt reminder of why she so actively disliked the man.

Not that there was any point brooding on the inevitable, she thought now, eyes fixed on the drive with all the nervous desperation of someone awaiting the hangman's noose. She had taken up position on the faded rust-coloured chair an hour before, when walking around the house had ceased to work as an effective courage-boosting exercise, and had not moved from her vigilant vantage point since. She reasoned that, if she had time to adjust to the sight of him before he swooped through the front door, then she might have a chance of steeling herself for his unpleasant impact.

In all events, the ploy didn't work because the minute the taxi swept up the drive every semblance of calm evaporated like a puff of smoke and her stomach went into immediate spasm.

In her limited dealings with Bruno Giannella, the one thing that Katy had always found supremely unfair was that power, wealth and intelligence could be harnessed together with such good looks. He deserved to be physically unfortunate. Or at least average. Instead, he had the sort of sensational dark looks that made women's heads snap round in stunned appreciation. Dark, glossy hair, the same colour as his eyes, a wide, sensual mouth and a bone structure that seemed to have been carved with a loving hand and an eye to perfection.

To Katy's mind, though, his scarily beautiful face was stamped with permanent coldness, his eyes were remote and detached and his mouth was cruelly forbidding.

When, shortly after she had begun working with Joseph, he had told her with a certain amount of grudging pride that his godson was quite something to be reckoned with when it came to the opposite sex, Katy had kept silent and wondered whether she was the only one who was immune to his so called legendary charm.

She watched Bruno furtively as he paid the taxi driver, picked up his overnight bag and his designer briefcase and then turned to look frowningly at the house. From a distance, Katy could almost kid herself that the man was made of flesh and blood. He moved, he spoke, he made mountains of money and was apparently a respected employer. And, of course, he adored his godfather. That much emotion she had caught in his eyes on the couple of occasions when she had been around him at the house. He couldn't be all bad.

Then the insistent jabbing on the doorbell shattered the illusion and Katy scuttled towards the front door to let him in. The minute she clapped eyes on him, she knew how she would feel. Gauche, awkward, unbearably plain and dowdy.

In fact, as she pulled open the door her eyes inadvertently slid away from the potently masculine figure towering in front of her and she cleared her throat nervously.

'Come in, Bruno. It's…good to see you.' She stood back so that he could brush past her, barely bothering to glance in her direction. 'How was your trip over? Okay?' Katy shut the front door and leaned against it for a bit of support.

Bruno strode into the hallway, took a little time out to absorb the atmosphere of the house—appropriately it was 'The Old School', considering his godfather had been a professor—before swinging round to confront the figure huddling against the front door.

If there was one thing that irritated the hell out of Bruno, it was to see someone cowering in front of him—and Katy West was cowering. Her brown curly hair was effectively hiding her downturned face and her hands were pressed behind her as if prepared at any given minute, to yank open the front door and hurtle down the path.

'We have to talk,' he said flatly, with the insouciance of someone accustomed to giving orders, speaking his mind and being obeyed, 'and I do not intend to stand here to conduct the conversation, so why don't you unglue yourself from the door and perhaps get us both a cup of tea?'

Joseph sang her praises to high heaven and, for the life of him, Bruno couldn't understand why. The girl hardly ever muttered a word. If she had a sparkling, intelligent personality then she always took great care to keep it well hidden whenever he was around. He almost clicked his tongue in irritation as she slid past him towards the kitchen.

'So,' he said as soon as they were in the kitchen, 'tell me what happened. And leave nothing out.' He sat down heavily on one of the kitchen chairs and watched as she stuck some water on to boil and fetched two mugs from the dresser.

It felt peculiar to be here, without his godfather around. Bruno didn't like it. For all his high-flying lifestyle, his apartments in Paris, London and New York, this house represented the one constant in his life and his godfather was an integral part of it. The thought that he might be more seriously ill than he imagined, that he might die, filled him with the chill of dread.

Which did not predispose him to be any kinder to the slip of a girl busying herself with the tea.

'When *exactly* did…did this thing happen?'

'I told you on the phone. Yesterday.' Katy had no need to look at him to feel his eyes boring into her.

'And could you look at me when I am talking to you? It's impossible having a conversation to someone who insists on speaking into her mug of tea!'

Katy duly looked at him and immediately felt unsteady. 'He had just had his tea…'

'What?'

'I said, Joseph had just finished—'

'No, no, no,' Bruno waved her aside impatiently. 'I mean *what* did he have for his tea? Anything that could be seen to have brought on this…attack? Are they quite sure that it was a heart attack? And not something else? Like food poisoning?'

'Of course they're sure! They're doctors, for heaven's sake!'

'Which is not to say that they're gods. Everyone's fallible.' He sipped some of his tea and then restlessly began loosening his tie, dragging it down a bit so that he could undo the top two buttons of his shirt.

Katy watched him with the morbid fascination of

someone watching something dangerous and unpredictable. Like a cobra snake.

'It wasn't food poisoning,' she said, remembering what he had said about her talking into the mug of tea and making a determined effort not to encourage further criticism. 'He literally had some bread that Maggie and I had baked earlier and a pot of tea. He was fine eating it, but then he said that he felt a bit odd, that he needed to go and lie down.' Katy could feel her eyes beginning to fill up at the memory of him, as the odd feeling had manifested itself as something rather more sinister. The way he had staggered and clutched his chest, barely able to get his words out.

'For God's sake, *don't cry*! It's enough dealing with what's happened without you blubbing!'

'Sorry,' she mumbled. 'It's just that I was so scared when…when it all happened. It was so unexpected…I know Joseph is nearly seventy, but really that isn't very old, is it? Not these days.' She had given up on the tea, which she hadn't really wanted anyway, and was twisting her hands nervously on her lap. At least he wouldn't be able to see that and lay into her for being emotional. 'And there'd been no sign of anything…just the day before we had gone on a walk in the gardens. To the greenhouse. He's terribly proud of his orchids. He inspects them every day. Talks to them sometimes.'

'I know,' Bruno said gruffly. Joseph wrote to him regularly once a week, always to his London address where his letters would be efficiently forwarded to whichever part of the world Bruno happened to be occupying at that moment. He had tried his utmost to bring him up to date with computer technology, had pointed out the numerous advantages of email, but, while his godfather had nodded indulgently and exclaimed in apparent awe at what computers were capable of doing, he still persisted in the old-fashioned way of communication. Bruno would stake his life that the spanking, up-to-the-minute computer he had bought for his godfather was still sitting in his den, unused and gathering dust.

Bruno knew all about Joseph's orchids and the various afflictions they had suffered over time. He knew all about what was happening in the village. He knew all about Katy West and how invaluable she had been over the past eighteen months in his employment.

'There must have been signs...' he insisted, shoving the mug to one side and further rattling Katy by leaning forward with his arms on the table.

'Nothing. I would have told you if there had been anything, anything that could have been seen as a warning...'

'Would you?' Anxiety about his godfather lent his voice a cynical harshness. Bruno Giannella was not accustomed to the uneasy panic that was sloshing through his system at the moment. The circumstances of his life had taught him from an early age that control was one of the most important steps to success. To control one's life, he privately maintained, was to hold it in the palm of one's hand.

'What do you mean?'

'I mean,' he said, standing up and prowling through the homely kitchen like a tiger suddenly released from its leash, 'I haven't exactly been flooded with information from you on how my godfather has been doing, have I? In fact...' he paused and cocked his head to one side consideringly '...I have never received so much as a single piece of communication from you on the subject of Joseph! Despite the fact that I made it patently clear when you were employed that keeping me informed of my godfather's well being was part and parcel of the deal!'

'That's not fair!' A sudden spurt of disbelieving anger made her cheeks redden at his accusation. 'I work for Joseph, and I don't…I don't think it's right to expect me to run behind his back to you with tales.'

She expected him to continue haranguing her, but instead Bruno grunted and resumed his unsettling prowl around the kitchen. Much more of this and Katy thought that she might well be joining Joseph in the hospital with an attack of overstretched nerves.

'And what is the hospital like?' Bruno demanded suddenly so that she was startled out of her temporary reverie on her malfunctioning nervous system.

'It's very good, Bruno. I went up there this morning and they wouldn't let me see him yet, but I've been told that his condition is stable.'

'Well, that's something, I suppose. How far from here is it?'

'About forty minutes' drive. Depends on the traffic getting into the town centre. I was told that it should be okay to go and see him later.'

'We'll leave here at four thirty in that case.'

Katy nodded and wondered whether this might be the right time to broach the question that had been plaguing her from the very minute he had informed her in that arrogant way of his that he would be flying over. Namely how long he intended staying.

He was already heading for the door by the time she gathered her senses together and half ran after him, only slowing down when she came to the hall.

'So…' she said brightly, keeping her distance as he reached down for the overnight bag. Not a very big bag, she was reassured to see.

'Yes?' Dark brows winged up as Bruno registered her hovering presence.

'You're…you're in the usual room. You know. Top of the stairs, turn left, end of the corridor! I've…I've put out a towel for you…' She stepped forward hesitantly. 'The thing is…'

'Spit it out, Katy.'

'Well, the thing is…I mean Maggie and I were wondering…well, just how long you intend to stay. I mean,' she rushed on as mild curiosity deepened into a frown of growing disapproval, 'it would really be helpful to her in terms of, well…you know, getting food in and such like.' She could feel her face getting more and more flushed as he heard out her stammering speech in utter silence.

'You needn't go to any trouble for me,' Bruno informed her, turning away and heading up the stairs while Katy watched him with the dawning realisation that he had failed to answer the one question that she desperately wanted answered.

With a spurt of uncustomary courage, she sprinted up the stairs in his wake and arrived slightly out of breath at his bedroom door just in time to see him dump the bag on the bed and dispose of his tie, which he tossed on top of the bag.

'Well?' With a sigh of impatience, he turned to her and began unbuttoning his shirt.

Katy kept her eyes fixed very firmly on his face and pointedly away from the slither of bronzed torso that his casual action was revealing.

'It's just that…' she cleared her throat and looked down at the tips of her brown loafers '…if you intend staying on…you know, it would be helpful if you could let me know what you expect of me…' In the deadly silence that greeted this faltering question, she became horrifyingly aware of connotations that she hadn't intended and a wave of mortification swept over her. 'I mean in terms of cooking for you,' she hurried on. 'Joseph and I were accustomed to having breakfast and lunch together. I—'

'Why do you do that?'

'I beg your pardon?' She stole a look at him and was dismayed to see that he had now removed his shirt entirely so that avoiding a full view of his muscular chest was out of the question.

'Why do you insist on acting like the hired help? Slouching as though your dearest wish is for the ground to open up and swallow you?'

'I *am* the hired help,' Katy said, folding her arms and forcing herself not to be intimidated by his suffocating presence.

'In the strictest form of the word,' he returned swiftly, 'but you're also Joseph's companion and apparently a very valuable part of his life. Despite my initial…shall we say, misgivings…it seems that you've exceeded my expectations.' He sounded faintly surprised at that. 'As such you do not exactly fall into the category of servant, so stop behaving like one. There is no need to concern yourself with fixing any meals for me while I am here,' he continued in the same clipped voice that made her want to salute smartly to attention. 'I am quite capable of doing my own thing.'

'Joseph would be appalled if he thought that…that you were having to take time off work because of him,' Katy said truthfully. What she didn't add was that his godfather was in awe of this gifted and charismatic man whom he had raised from adolescence.

'He would be equally appalled if he thought that I couldn't spare him the time when he needed me. Now is there anything else?'

For someone who had to be very perceptive—or how

else could he have ever achieved the dizzy heights of power that he had?—it amazed Katy that he could on the one hand criticise her for behaving like a servant, while on the other, treating her exactly like one.

'No,' she mumbled, blushing furiously as she noticed his hand move to the leather belt of his trousers. He wasn't going to remove it, was he? How far would he go in his stripping-off before he became embarrassed by her presence?

Katy's knowledge of men was seriously limited. In twenty-three-years, she had had two boyfriends, both thoroughly nice young men for whom she had felt great affection. It was a mark of her basic friendship with them that she still kept in touch with both.

She couldn't imagine either of them casually undressing in front of a woman they didn't know from Adam.

'Right.' Bruno's voice was dismissive. 'In that case, I'll see you downstairs at four-thirty precisely.' He turned away from the shrinking figure and was only aware that she had gone when he heard the door close quietly with a click behind her.

In between her irritating, agonised mumblings, the girl had raised a very good point and one that Bruno himself had considered on the trip over.

His work. There was no way that he could think about paying his godfather a cursory visit. Joseph was the one human being in the entire world who meant something to him. It pained him to realise how little he had actually seen him over the past year. He could only count a handful of times, fleeting visits when he could manage to escape from the tyranny of his working life. If he vanished now and his godfather, God forbid, died, Bruno knew that he would never forgive himself.

He could use his London apartment and work from the

offices in the City, he supposed, but even that would entail an involved commute.

He chewed over the problem while he had a bath. Despite being on the go for the better part of a day, the thought of catching up on some sleep before they left did not inspire him. Sleep, on the whole, always seemed like something that had to be done, but was essentially a waste of time. The only attraction he had ever seen in a bed usually involved the woman lying on it and it had to be said that, however fulfilling the sex was, it was never enough to keep him wallowing under a duvet cover so that he could indulge in post-coital chit-chat.

By the time he had changed and run through some emails, he had already worked out a solution to his problem. It wasn't ideal, he reflected as he took in the hovering figure waiting for him in the hall when he emerged from his room an hour and a half later, but it would have to do.

'Jimbo's got the Range Rover out of the garage.' Katy rushed into speech as Bruno shrugged on his jacket. It was May. Sunny but with a chill in the air that promised goose-pimples to anyone hardy enough to walk around in short sleeves. Katy thought, with a certain amount of sourness, that Bruno had typically got his dress code exactly right. Tan trousers, checked shirt and a suede jacket that managed to look well worn and authentically beaten as well as incredibly fashionable and hideously expensive. How did he do that? Look rugged and sophisticated at the same time?

She felt the familiar rush of self-consciousness as she took in her own dress code, which was a grey stretch skirt reaching to her calves, a baggy beige jumper and her thoroughly un-chic grey cord jacket. He always made her feel so horribly awkward. All year round, she felt very comfortable in these clothes. They were functional, hard-wearing and successfully managed to conceal a figure she felt self-conscious about and was constantly reminded about whenever she was in his presence.

'Jimbo?' Bruno paused to frown and Katy nodded.

'Jim Parks, the man who looks after the garden and does odd jobs around the house. You've met him.'

'I'll take your word for it.' If he had, then he didn't remember.

'Anyway, the car's waiting outside. If you like, I'll drive.' To her dismay, he nodded.

Katy was a good driver and she was accustomed to driving Joseph's car. She regularly went into the town once a week on her afternoon off to shop and she drove Joseph wherever he wanted, which admittedly wasn't to anywhere far flung, but she had become used to the old gears. Several times she had even used the car to drive down to Cornwall to spend the weekend with her parents.

None of that made her any the less nervous as she switched on the engine and started down the drive with Bruno's intense black eyes watching her every move. It was like taking her driving test all over again, except worse. At least her driving test examiner had been a kindly man in his fifties who had put her at her ease, not an arrogant half-Italian who wouldn't hesitate to launch into a scathing attack on her competence if she happened to change gears a little too roughly.

She could barely concentrate on his reasonably polite line of conversation as he asked her about traffic in the town centre and about how she amused herself on her days off. She was just too aware of him looking at her to relax.

She was releasing a long sigh of relief at the sight of

the hospital in the distance when he threw her his bombshell.

'I have been thinking about what you said to me about taking time off work and I agree that Joseph would be unhappy if he thought I was forcing myself to stay here, twiddling my thumbs, because I felt sorry for him.'

Katy glanced surreptitiously at him, then quickly back at the congested road that harboured a plethora of small roundabouts and traffic lights before veering right towards the hospital entrance. The fact that he had actually thought about anything she had said was surprising enough without the additional bonus of knowing that he had agreed with her on something.

'Yes, he really would.' She breathed a little sigh of relief at what she knew was coming. His imminent departure. But first he wanted her to go through the motions of soothing away his guilt. 'He's terribly proud, you know. He would hate to think that you felt sorry enough for him to let your…well, your work life slide.' She frowned and tried to imagine what it must be like to live a life where everything and everyone came a poor second to work. 'You have an apartment in London, don't you?'

'Of course I have,' Bruno said irritably. 'Look at the state of this car park. We'll be here for hours trying to find a space. You should have told me that the parking facilities were inadequate. I would have arranged for a taxi to bring us here.'

'We'll find somewhere to park,' Katy mumbled, scanning the clutter of cars for a vacant spot to back up her optimistic statement. 'We just have to be patient.'

Bruno clicked his tongue in instant dismissal of such a notion and frowned darkly out of his window. 'A much overrated virtue, patience. Wait too long for something and it's guaranteed to disappear before you can get your hands on it. If I patiently waited for deals to come my way, I would be struggling to put a crust on the table.'

'But we're not talking about deals, Bruno. We're talking about finding a parking space in a car park.' Her eyes brightened as she spotted someone reversing slowly out of a slot in the lane parallel to hers and she cautiously inched the car forward so that she could ease it into the vacated spot. 'There,' she said with satisfaction. 'didn't I tell you we'd get something?'

'I was telling you about my...dilemma...concerning work,' Bruno answered, sweeping over her small victory so that Katy instantly felt deflated.

'Oh, yes. Perhaps we could discuss it after we've been to see your godfather?' She could already feel her spirits lifting at the thought of seeing Joseph. That he had come to mean so much to her in the space of a mere eighteen months was of no great surprise to Katy. As an only child, she had always had a gift when it came to relating to people older than herself and Joseph was somehow special. His blend of shyness, intelligence and gentleness had charmed her from the very first minute she had met him and she had never had any cause to revise her opinions. She was as much at home with him when they were having heated discussions on some subject or other that might have captured his interest in the news, as when they were sitting in companionable silence at the end of the evening before he retired to bed.

She hoped that he would be able to see them now and perhaps even chat a little and she would much rather relish her anticipation in peaceful silence than be forced to respond to the man striding alongside her.

'We'll discuss it now, I think,' Bruno informed her crushingly. He pushed open the glass door and then stood aside to let her pass. 'I want to focus on Joseph when I see him, knowing that I have sorted out this work situation to my satisfaction. In fact—' he glanced around '—there must be some kind of coffee shop or café or something here. I should have said what I need to say in fifteen minutes and then we can go and see Joseph.'

Katy fought down an urge to salute. She also knew better than to express an alternative viewpoint so she suggested the café that was further along on the ground floor. The coffee was fairly awful but they would be able to sit and, anyway, it made sense for her to do what she had to do, nod when he told her that he would be going down to London so that he could carry on working and agree that it was really the only viable solution. At least that way she, too, would feel a weight lifted with the matter sorted.

'What will you have?' Bruno asked, not looking at her as he assumed his place in the short queue, his hand squarely placed on top of one of the brown trays.

Somehow direct questions from Bruno always managed to encourage a stammer that Katy possessed with no one else. Of course, when she thought about it, she could understand why. Even when he was being perfectly normal, if such a thing existed in connection with his personality, there was still a latent aggression to him that brought out the worst in her.

'Hello?' she heard him saying now, finally turning to look at her so that for an instant their eyes tangled and a slow, hot burn started inside her. 'Is there anyone there? Or have you decided to vanish into the clouds completely?'

'Sorry,' Katy said, blinking and looking away. 'I'll have a coffee.'

'Anything to eat?'

'No. Thank you. Thanks.'

Frowning black eyes did a once-over sweep of her, finally coming to rest on her flushed face. 'How much do you eat? Does Joseph make sure that you get fed properly? He can be a little absent-minded when it comes to life's small essentials. Like food.' He was at the coffee machine now, pressing buttons for two cups of coffee, while Katy looked on in bewilderment at the turn in his conversation.

'Of course I eat.' She eyed the restful solitude of one of the tables wistfully.

'You look like a bag of bones under that outfit of yours.'

In one fell swoop, he managed to make her cringingly aware of her body and its shortcomings. Ever since she was fourteen and had watched on the sidelines as her friends had developed hips and breasts and all the things that the boys seemed to gravitate towards, Katy had nursed the unspoken feeling that her slightness, her small breasts, her boyish shape, were to be concealed at all costs. Baggy, all-enveloping clothes had become her preferred mode of dress, even though her parents had repeatedly told her that she was beautiful. She had always known better than to believe them. Her parents adored her. They would have found her beautiful if she had had three heads and a tail.

Now she knew that she should greet his uninvited observation with something icily scathing, something that would firmly put him in his place, but nothing came to mind and in the brief silence he continued with bracing disregard for her feelings.

'You need to build yourself up.'

'Build myself up into *what*? A wrestler?' Katy said with a spurt of vigour and this time he looked at her with something approaching interest, his dark eyebrows raised in apparent fascination at her sudden forceful tone of voice.

'I really don't know, now that you mention it, considering you keep your body so cleverly concealed under clothing that any granny would be proud to wear,' Bruno answered smoothly, but her sarcasm had captured his attention and suddenly the plans he had made regarding work didn't seem quite so depressingly functional after all.

'Now, we'll have our coffee and I'll tell you exactly what I've decided on the work front. Why don't you go and grab a table—a clean one would be good—and I'll join you when I've paid for this lot?'

He absent-mindedly watched as Katy scuttled across the café to one of the tables at the back, but his thoughts were already moving ahead. He couldn't see that she would object in any way to what he had in mind and, quite frankly, she had no choice in the matter anyway.

However, his problems did not begin and end with work. Isobel Hutton Smith, the woman with whom he was currently attached, might have been a model of understanding when it came to his frequent trips abroad, but he doubted whether she would be quite so compliant when it came to him holed up in the countryside a good hour and a half away from her, yet in the same country.

She had been dropping hints about him settling in one place for good, spicing up her conversation with all-too-transparent musings about the nature of relationships and the speed with which time rushed past.

Bruno knew that he should have been firmer in squashing some of her more blatant chat about commitment and biological clocks, but somehow he had never seemed to get around to it and he'd allowed the situation to slide. Maybe, he thought now, Joseph's illness was fate telling him that the time to settle down had arrived, and as he distractedly paid the girl at the till for the two coffees and the tired-looking Chelsea bun he had bought for himself he wondered whether Isobel might not make just the sort of wife he was looking for. Glamorous, well connected and undemanding when it came to his work.

He glanced across to where Katy now appeared to be brushing a few wayward crumbs from the surface of the table with her hand and decided that he would deal with one thing at a time.

Work first, girlfriend later and both in second position to the all-consuming need to make sure that his godfather was going to be all right.

CHAPTER TWO

'RIGHT.' Bruno sat down, brilliant black eyes sweeping over the grubby table with such unconcealed distaste that Katy was forced to remind him that a hospital canteen wasn't going to be along the lines of a five-star restaurant.

'I did try to clear most of the crumbs,' she finished apologetically, which earned her a frown.

'Why are you apologising for the state of this place?' Bruno demanded impatiently. 'Nobody, least of all me, expects a hospital café to be run along the lines of a five-star restaurant, but this table looks as though its ambition is to collect several months of grime before someone gets round to wiping a damp cloth over it.'

Katy wondered how his employees coped with his obviously impossibly high standards. Did he pour that undiluted, freezing scorn over anyone who happened to make the smallest slip-up? She shuddered and gulped down a mouthful of coffee.

How his godfather's gentleness and sensitivity had never managed to rub off on him baffled Katy. He was as different from Joseph as chalk from cheese, but then she knew that his family background had not been normal. His father had died when he was three and his mother ten years later, during which time he had had the pleasure of being sent to a boarding-school, when he was just a child and not old enough to cross a road by himself let alone cope with being sent away from the only home he had known. He had also had the dubious pleasure of being at the mercy of two stepfathers, neither of whom, from what she had gathered, had been very interested in the precociously intelligent but rebellious child.

By the time he had reached Joseph, at the age of thirteen, his personality had probably already been formed. He'd been an orphan, wealthy thanks to his mother's legacy, formidably clever and, according to his godfather, well on the way to believing that the world was at his command.

Reading between the lines, Katy could picture a devilishly good-looking teenager, cleverer than most of his teachers, fiercely self-confident, yet wary of human relationships.

She often tried to bolster her self-confidence in his presence by thinking of him as rather lonely underneath the glittering success and financial power.

Yet again, the ploy failed as she surreptitiously glanced at his darkly striking features as he bit down into the flaccid bun.

'You were going to tell me what…what you've decided to do? About work?' Katy prompted.

'Well, I won't be returning to New York, at least not until Joseph is back on his feet. The obvious solution would be for me to concentrate on my London office and stay in my apartment in Chelsea, but that in itself would involve a hectic commute if I wanted to get up here to see him, so I've decided that the only solution will be for me to set up an office at the house and work from there indefinitely.'

'House? What house?' Katy wondered whether she had missed some vital connecting link somewhere in what he had said.

'What house do you think?' Bruno's tone was exaggeratedly patient, the tone of someone who had to slow down the natural pace of his mind to accommodate the sluggishness of someone else's. Hers. He fixed his fabulous dark eyes on her startled face and watched as comprehension gathered pace.

'You're going to work from *Joseph's house*?' Katy squeaked. Her stomach seemed to be doing a frantic tapdance inside her. Thank God she was sitting down or else she might have keeled over at the horrifying prospect now unfolding before her eyes.

'Correct. Now drink up, we can't spend all day here discussing this.'

Her eyes were as wide as saucers as she looked at him. Yes, of course she had anticipated that he would be around for a couple of days, a week at the most, and she had already decided that if that was the case, then she could quite easily avoid him. It was a big house. With a bit of forward planning she need never run into him, and on the few occasions when avoidance was out of the question she would just take a deep breath and cope with the temporary discomfort.

But *an indefinite stay*?

'Furthermore—' Bruno flicked his wrist so that he could glance at his watch '—you'll be working for me. It's not ideal. I would have preferred someone with a bit more experience in dealing with the business world, but you're available and you'll have to do. I can't very well ask my own secretary to uproot herself and move up here to accommodate me. Not when she has a husband and two children to consider.' The implication being that, were it not for those emotional anchors, he would have had no hesitation at all in uprooting her.

'There's really no need to look so stricken, Katy. I don't bite.' He stood up and she realised that, as far as he was concerned, the conversation was over. Not that it had even *been* a conversation. He had informed her of what he intended to do and her duty was to keep quiet and oblige.

And as she tripped along behind him, watching blankly as he charmed the nurses on duty and headed down the corridor for Joseph's room, all she could think of was the nightmare prospect of what he had just proposed.

She would have to have it out with him, she thought feverishly. In an ideal world, she would not have had to communicate with him at all, but she would just have to bite the bullet and confront him with the impossibility of his suggestion. Not that it had been couched as such.

She found that her pleasure at seeing Joseph was considerably dimmed by the metaphorical cleaver she now felt to be hanging over her neck.

It hardly helped that after a few minutes during which she held Joseph's hand while Bruno toyed with something approaching a bedside manner, the subject of her new role was foisted onto her clearly still weak employer.

'I really don't think that this is the time…' Katy initiated a hesitant protest and Bruno quelled her with a glance.

'I am simply reassuring my godfather that he can count on my being around for the foreseeable future.'

'You mustn't interrupt your work schedule,' Joseph predictably objected, then, to her dismay, he continued wanly, 'though, of course, it would be very nice for me to know that you'll be at the house, looking after it, so to speak, and looking after my dear Katy as well…'

Katy tried not to splutter at this.

'I do *not* need looking after, Joseph,' she managed to say with a lot of commendable self-control and keeping her eyes very pointedly averted from Bruno's intense, unsettling gaze. 'I'm nearly twenty-four! I think it's fair to say that I'm perfectly capable of looking after myself, and of making sure that the house doesn't fall down around my ears! Besides,' she said encouragingly, giving his hand a little squeeze, 'you'll be home sooner than you think.'

'Is that what the doctor says?'

'Well, no, not exactly, but then we haven't actually spoken to any doctors as yet—'

'Typically there's never a doctor around when you need one,' Bruno interrupted, scowling darkly. 'Apparently he won't be surfacing for another hour and I've given the nurse strict instructions that he's to see me before he begins his rounds.'

Joseph met Katy's eyes in a moment of mutual understanding. She wondered whether it had even occurred to Bruno that a busy doctor might not appreciate being summoned by a relative of one of his patients, and then decided that it probably hadn't. Bruno simply assumed that his wishes would be obeyed, supposedly for no other reason than the fact that he had been the one to issue them.

It would be a salutary lesson to him if he found himself at the bottom of the pecking order when Joseph's consultant arrived. Katy found herself drifting off into a pleasant day-dream in which Bruno was forced to wait at the end of a long queue shuffling along a corridor while, at the head of the line, a consultant as domineering as Bruno took his time while Bruno frantically tried to commandeer his attention from the back. She made the puppet figure in her head jump up and down in frustrated indignation and discovered she was smiling when Bruno's voice brought her plunging back to reality.

'Are you with us?' he asked, short-circuiting all politeness as usual, and Katy sat up a little straighter.

'I was just thinking...'

'Well, we'd better be heading off. Joseph needs his

rest…' They both looked at the old man, whose eyes had drooped.

'He looks so frail,' Katy whispered in sudden anguish. She turned impulsively to Bruno only to collide with cold black eyes.

'What would you expect?' He stood up and strode over to the door where he waited restlessly for her. 'He has had a heart attack,' he continued harshly. 'Did you imagine you would find him performing cartwheels?'

'No, but—'

'And I don't think it's very helpful,' Bruno continued, preceding her to the door and then allowing her to brush past him into the corridor, 'for you to let him see that there's any doubt that he'll have a full recovery and be back to his usual self.'

'I didn't!' Katy protested in a dismayed whisper. 'I mean, he couldn't hear what I said and…and he wasn't looking at me. In fact, he had nodded off! Of course, I wouldn't want him to imagine that…that well…'

'Where is this doctor?' Bruno was scanning the corridor, as out of place as a fish in a tree. Katy could see the scurrying nurses glancing at him with interest as he frowningly surveyed the scene.

'I don't think it's been an hour yet,' Katy said dubiously. 'Maybe we should just sit and wait.'

Bruno looked at her as though the concept of sitting and waiting for anything or anyone was a foreign concept that he could not compute.

'Standing here isn't going to make the consultant appear any quicker,' she pointed out tentatively. 'And we're getting in the way.'

Before he had time to come back at her with one of his biting responses, Katy walked off towards one of the nurses at the desk and politely asked whether they could be notified of the consultant's arrival when he appeared so that they could have a quick word.

'His godson is very worried,' she murmured in a low voice, while Bruno breathed down her neck in a very off-putting manner.

'His godson is understandably anxious to have a few answers,' Bruno interjected with a show of perfect politeness, and Katy wondered how he managed to sound so threatening when he was delivering, for him, quite an inoffensive remark. She had no need to look at him. She could imagine the unsmiling expression on his face all too clearly. The nurse must have picked up the same signals as well because the bland, bordering on bossy expression he'd worn had been replaced by a nervous nodding of the head.

'If I kept people sitting and waiting all day long,' was the first thing he muttered as soon as they had sat on the functional chairs further along the corridor, 'I would no longer be in business.'

Katy discreetly held her tongue as there was no point in antagonising him when she still had to raise the sensitive subject still making her ill.

'And just let me do the talking when this consultant makes his appearance,' he grated. 'Tiptoeing around the man isn't going to get the answers that I need!'

Katy sneaked a sidelong glance at him and knew, with blinding certainty, that Bruno was worried, desperately worried, and the only way he could deal with it was to become even more aggressive and forceful than he normally was. Her heart went out to him and on impulse she placed her small hand on his wrist, only to find him stare at it with such concentrated distaste that she immediately removed it.

'Oh, spare me the compassion, Katy.'

'Do you ever let that guard down, Bruno?' she heard herself asking and immediately realised that she had overstepped the boundary. Personal questions like that were not encouraged by a man like him. Even Joseph shied away from indulging his curiosity about his godson's life, only letting slip now and again to her questions that clearly nagged away at him.

'Sorry,' she apologised immediately. 'None of my business. We're both worried.'

She waited for him to fill the brief pause, which he didn't, and Katy released a little sigh. She thought that he had relegated her remark to oblivion and was surprised when he said in a low, musing voice, 'Joseph has never been ill. Not with anything serious anyway. It's odd but you never imagine that the people you care about are ever vulnerable; you foolishly imagine that they're going to somehow live for ever.'

Katy discovered that she was sitting on the edge of her chair and holding her breath. She felt a flood of sympathy at his unexpected admission but knew better than to express it. His moment of weakness would pass and then he would look back and resent her for having witnessed it in the first place.

'I wondered,' she volunteered hesitantly, 'if we could discuss this work thing, Bruno...'

Bruno inclined his body slightly so that he was looking at her, eyes narrowed. It took all the will-power at her disposal not to look away and thereby earn his irritation. Hadn't he already snapped at her that he found it impossible to conduct a conversation with someone who couldn't meet his eyes? How was he supposed to know that one glance in her direction was sufficient to reduce her to a state of panic?

'What's there to talk about?' he asked in a reasonable voice.

'I...I really haven't got the right qualifications to work for you,' Katy stuttered. 'I mean, I've never worked as a professional secretary or anything...'

He frowned. 'You're helping Joseph with his memoirs, aren't you?'

'Well, yes, but...'

'And correct me if I'm wrong, but that must involve at least some of the usual things, such as an ability to type.'

'Well, yes, I *know* how to type, but—'

'I thought you'd taken a course—'

'A very *short* course,' Katy swiftly pointed out. 'I mean, I was a nanny for four years and when the Harrisons found that they would be moving abroad they helped me out by sending me on a three-month sort of crash course so that I could help Joseph out with odd bits of typing.' She licked her lips nervously and discovered that, far from wanting to look away, she was mesmerised by her close-up view of his lean, strong face and the way the weak sunlight filtering through the windows highlighted the blackness of his hair.

'Why did they do that?' he asked, frowning.

'Oh, they liked me. I still keep in touch with them, you know.'

'And as a token of their affection, they decided to send you on a secretarial course? You're losing me here, Katy.'

'Well, I mentioned that I wanted to break away from nannying. Not,' she stressed, 'that I didn't enjoy every minute of it. I did! I was looking after two lovely children and really I couldn't have wished for a better start to life in London. The Harrisons were the perfect employers. I mean, so is Joseph, to be honest. I've been very lucky…'

'Katy—' he shook his head in fascinated bemusement '—where is this going? I didn't ask for a potted history of your working life. I simply wanted to know why you were objecting to working for me.'

'Right. Yes, well, what I was saying was that working on Joseph's memoirs isn't like being a *real* secretary.' In a minute he would say that she was losing him again. She could see it in his expression. He wanted her to get to the point and not be sidetracked by a long ramble. 'I do a little bit of typing, but not a huge amount. Mostly I take some dictation, very, very slowly, and then when Joseph goes off to have his nap I type it up. Very, very slowly.' She felt obliged to get the picture straight. 'He doesn't work at breakneck speed, Bruno.'

Bruno smiled with genuine amusement at that and she found that she was even more mesmerised by that smile.

'I won't be able to keep up with you,' Katy said bluntly. 'And I don't expect that you have a lot of patience for mistakes. I make a lot of mistakes. I spend ages correcting them.' In case he wasn't getting the very pointed message, she decided to leave him in no doubt of her unsuitability. 'In fact it usually takes me as long to correct my mistakes as it does to type the thing up in the first place. I'm not clever with computers and Joseph doesn't mind one bit because he's absolutely hopeless with them as well.'

'You should have a bit more confidence in yourself,' Bruno informed her bracingly. 'And familiarity with computers is just a question of practice.'

'I have lots of confidence in myself,' Katy denied as she saw the lifebelt of her professed incompetence slipping out of her grasp. 'Just not when it comes to technology. You could hire a temp from one of the agencies in town. There are loads of them floating around! Someone with that business experience you mentioned earlier!'

'But then, what would you do all day long?' Bruno looked at her narrowly. 'You *are* being paid, after all, and with Joseph in hospital there would be nothing for you to do, would there? Instead of jumping to the conclusion that you would never be able to work for me, you should think of it as a challenge to fill in the long hours in an empty house.'

A challenge? Shouldn't a challenge be something that someone looked forward to? Who ever looked at something they were horrified at doing and saw it as a *challenge*? Did this man inhabit the same planet as the rest of the human race?

Before she could contemplate what he had said and return with something adequate, however, the consultant arrived and the next half an hour was spent with her listening while Bruno took over the reins of the conversation. He asked questions she would never have thought of with a bluntness that she was personally mortified by but which the consultant seemed to appreciate, judging from the hearty, informative depths of his replies.

The upshot was that there was absolutely no reason why Joseph shouldn't make a full recovery. He should even be encouraged to do a bit of light exercise, and he would be back at the house within a couple of weeks or so. As a mark of how much Bruno had impressed him, he even scribbled his home number on a piece of paper and told them both that they could reach him any time if they had any more questions or were worried about anything.

'Exercise,' Bruno murmured, half to himself as they

headed out of the hospital towards the car. 'Joseph's only form of exercise is light walks in the garden, am I right?'

'He's no spring chicken, Bruno,' Katy said, and then, unable to resist a little dig, she added straight-faced, 'What would you expect him to do? Cartwheels round the flower beds?'

She was startled and irrationally pleased by the sudden burst of laughter that greeted this piece of tart sarcasm and it was only when they were in the car proceeding carefully out of the city and back towards the house that Katy remembered the unfinished conversation about work. Or, rather, unfinished from her point of view. Bruno had obviously decided that the subject matter was closed and was now thoughtfully ruminating on the challenges posed by the consultant in connection with the light exercise from which his godfather might benefit.

Katy took a deep breath and then burst out, 'But how can you run—is it an empire that you run?—from a *house*? I mean, don't you need to be there, *on standby*, just in case...' her voice trailed off as she tried to envisage the dynamics of big business '...just in case something *happens*?'

'Something like what?' Bruno asked curiously.

'I don't know exactly...' Katy said vaguely, frowning. 'Some catastrophe or something.'

'You mean like the building falling down?'

Katy read the amusement in his voice as a subversive attack on her obvious ignorance of corporate finance and the money-making business in which she had never had much interest.

'I mean,' she stressed bravely, 'don't you need to actually be in an office in your building so that if people have problems they can have...well, access to you? Face to face?'

'Oh, no,' Bruno drawled smoothly. 'Technology these days is actually quite sophisticated…'

'It's not my fault I've never been computer literate,' Katy muttered in defence. 'Of course, we *did* have IT lessons at school but I was never really interested. I've always thought that computers were so impersonal.' She peered thoughtfully out of the window straight ahead as she edged the car through the city traffic at a snail's pace, and considered her school life. Oh, she had been very happy there, but not in her most optimistic moments would she ever have described herself as one of those thrusting high achievers who seemed destined for the top careers. She had tried very hard to master the world of computer technology but she had never risen above pedestrian and it had never bothered her.

She couldn't see how she was going to get out of working for Bruno, especially when he had covered the underhand route of reminding her that she was being paid and would, presumably, be on call to him if his godfather wasn't physically around. But when she pictured herself speeding around with whirlwind efficiency, answering phones and rushing at his breakneck pace, her mind seemed to shut down and a sickish feeling began to rise up in the pit of her stomach. Maybe if she didn't feel so awkward and foolish in his company, she might have managed to pull off a passable show of competence, but the reality was that she would stumble over everything and end up enraging him.

Couldn't he see that? Why would he want to open himself up to endless irritation because she just wouldn't be able to keep up? Her mind flew off into a mortifying scenario in which her every mistake would be ridiculed until he had no option but to get someone in to replace her.

'Impersonal they may be, but they're also invaluable.'

'Huh?'

She sensed him take a deep indrawn breath of pure impatience.

'Computers,' Bruno reminded her heavily. 'We were talking about computers. Or rather *you* were. You were telling me that you were never interested in them at school?'

'Oh, yes. Sorry.'

'You have an unfortunate habit of apologising for everything,' Bruno remarked in the same heavy voice that made Katy think of teachers on the edge of losing their patience in the face of some particularly dim pupil. 'You'll have to lose that when you start working for me. It's annoying.'

'But what about when I make mistakes?' Katy asked worriedly.

'There you go. Assuming a worst-case scenario before we've even begun. What am I doing? Branching out on a completely irrelevant tangent!'

'But don't you find that happens?' Katy couldn't help saying. Now that she thought about it, she was *always* doing that! Joseph would start briskly enough with his dictating and then before you knew it a thousand questions rushed to her head and inevitably they ended up wildly off course. But how else did you ever find out about people if you just stuck to asking relevant questions?

'Computers? They allow me to work from pretty much anywhere. I can have my secretary email me my correspondence and I can access all the files I need at the press of a button. How do you imagine I continue running my London branch when I'm over in New York? And vice versa?'

'I can't,' Katy told him truthfully. They had finally managed to clear the bulk of the traffic and she relaxed as the roads became a little less congested. 'In fact, I can't imagine what you *do* at all. It must be very stressful.'

'I thrive under pressure.'

'Oh,' Katy murmured dubiously.

'At any rate, what I'm saying is that Joseph's office will do just fine in the short term. I'll probably spend a day or so in London—' he paused '—just in case I need to ward off any of those mysterious catastrophes you mentioned, but the rest of the week I'll spend here. I already have my laptop with me, as a matter of fact, so it should be no problem transferring files to Joseph's PC, and whatever clothes I have here will do for the time being.'

With her last limp objection thoroughly demolished, Katy slumped behind the driving wheel and dejectedly contemplated life ahead for the next fortnight. He had already started his list of personality traits she would have to change so that he could put up with her, and she was in no doubt that the list would grow until something resembling his specifications had been achieved.

She surfaced to hear him talking and realised that he was once more on the topic of light exercise and, at the mention of swimming, she glanced briefly in his direction. Just the sight of his frowning, averted profile sent a disturbing little shiver of awareness rippling through her. One more thing to contend with, she acknowledged dismally. He couldn't help the way he looked but that bronzed, dangerously beautiful face still managed to elicit a thoroughly uncharacteristically feminine response in her, even though she disliked him. She hoped against hope that a bout of close encounters would eliminate the unwanted reaction.

'Joseph doesn't like swimming,' she told him now. 'He once told me that if humans were made to flap about in water, they would have been born with gills. He doesn't find it a very soothing form of exercise.'

'I'm not suggesting that he swim across the Channel,' Bruno said. 'But swimming is gentle exercise and you heard what the doctor said.'

'Yes, but…that pool is in a state of total disrepair.'

'Because it's never used.'

'I'm surprised *you* don't use it when you come up to visit Joseph,' Katy reflected, thinking that, with his superbly fit build, he would have wanted to fling himself into any kind of exercise available whenever he had the odd moment of leisure. Thinking, too, how good he would look in swimming trunks. Bronzed body, not a spare ounce of flesh… She dragged her mind away from the rapidly growing image with a little twinge of guilt.

'It's too uncomfortable in there. It's also in dire need of renovation. It was pretty decrepit when Joseph moved in all those years ago and it's just got worse.' He paused. 'It would certainly benefit from a face-lift. I mean, thinking about it, it has all the essential requirements. It's indoors, even if you do have to exit the house to get to it, and with a bit of work it would be okay. I could get some form of heating installed, have a couple of changing rooms put in, bring someone in to repair the cracks everywhere…'

'It needs more than a face-lift,' Katy pointed out. 'Bruno, there are *weeds* growing out of the cracks at the bottom! In fact, the last time Joseph looked at it he suggested that with just the addition of a bit of soil we could convert the whole thing into a greenhouse!'

'Did he really say that?'

Katy nodded, glanced at him and in the diminishing light saw him grin with genuine amusement. For a second or two, her heart seemed to literally stop beating, then she refocused on the road in sudden, tumultuous confusion. Of course he wasn't responding to *her*, she told herself sternly. *She* evoked that icy, black-eyed impatience, but still…it was like seeing a sudden, dazzling ray of sun breaking through a bank of thunderclouds.

Then he was back to his usual self, the one she was accustomed to. Back to the man giving orders without bothering to tack on a *please* at the end or even display the slightest sign of appreciation.

'Well, we'll have to do something about changing his opinion, and that can be your first job in the morning. I'll head down to London for the day to get whatever I need from the office, so you'll have the day completely free to contact all the people you need to get that concrete hole up and running.'

'Up and running? How long do you imagine it's going to take to do that?'

'Throw enough money at them and it'll take just as long as I want it to take,' Bruno assured her. 'But it's to be finished before Joseph returns home. The last thing he needs is a series of workmen disturbing his peaceful recovery.'

'I'm not sure…'

'Number one lesson in the world of business is to *always* be sure,' Bruno informed her. 'Number two is to get them working to *your* tune. If you refuse to put up with delays and cancellations, you'll pretty much find that people will work to the timetable *you've* instructed them to work to!'

Katy almost repeated her heartfelt emotion that she

really wasn't sure at all, but bit back the words at the last minute. Instead she said doubtfully, 'I've never really had anyone work to my tune before…'

'So now you are to be provided with yet another challenge! And on the subject of the pool, I also think we ought to get some furniture for around it.'

'What sort of furniture?'

'Chairs. Comfortable ones. Chairs that Joseph can relax on when he's had a little bit of his gentle exercise. I'll leave the choice up to you. And don't breathe a word of this to him. It'll be a surprise.'

'Do you think his heart can stand it?'

'Are you being serious?'

'No,' Katy admitted. 'But once he's seen it, it might be an idea if we let him grow gradually into the concept of actually getting into it.'

They were finally approaching the house, which stood a way back from the road up a long, winding drive lined with trees. In a couple of months, the budding leaves would be thick and green and would almost obscure the red-brick house sprawling at the end of the drive. For the moment, though, there was just the merest hint of summer floating in the evening air, and as always Katy's heart revived at the sight of the old house shimmering into view. It also revived on the blessed thought that she had managed to drive into the city centre and out again, with Bruno as her passenger, without making a fool of herself. The least he could have done was to have thanked her for taking him, but naturally that would have been asking too much. He had launched into a succinct and off-putting summary of her forthcoming duties, next to which cajoling a workforce to accomplish the near impossible in his absence seemed like a bed of roses.

He strode into the house, switching on lights and briefing her on his expectations. He would be working from the house the day after tomorrow, he announced, and she should be ready to kick off no later than eight-thirty. He himself would be up and running by seven but, naturally, he would not expect her to conform so rigidly to his timetable. Breakfast he would see to himself and she could do her own thing for lunch, although he would expect her to eat on the run if there was a particularly heavy workload. He assumed that Maggie would see to their dinner requirements. Her working day would be expected to end by five-thirty.

Katy almost laughed out loud when he concluded his speech and politely asked her whether she had any questions, because he didn't look as though he was ready to sit down and actually respond to any. In fact, he was standing restlessly by the balustrade, like an engine throbbing on all cylinders and waiting to be revved into action.

Katy shook her head numbly and he gave her a curt nod.

'Good. In that case, I shall be in the office setting things up. Don't bother to wait for me for dinner. I'll grab something somewhere along the line, but I have a lot to think about and one or two overseas phone calls to make.'

Katy nodded again, deprived of speech, and felt tremendous sympathy for his poor secretary.

Thank goodness Joseph would be back soon and life could get back to normal.

CHAPTER THREE

BRUNO watched Katy through the sprawling bay window in the sitting room, from which he could see her standing in the brick outbuilding that had been converted into an indoor swimming pool by the original owners of the house. The doors were flung open and she had her back to him, hands propped against her waist as she supervised what he assumed were the industrious workmen he had instructed her to employ. The sleeves of her shapeless jumper were pushed up to the elbows and beneath the long skirt peeped a pair of sturdy green wellingtons.

It was after five and he'd just returned from the hospital having seen his godfather, who was making a good recovery.

'Food's terrible,' Joseph complained. 'Bland.' Then he looked a little sheepishly at Bruno. 'This work thing. You aren't going to impose your ridiculous work schedule on Katy, are you?'

'Ridiculous?'

'Well, you know what a workaholic you are...'

There was the faintest hint of disapproval in his voice that made Bruno squirm. 'Running a successful business can't be done if I spend all my time playing golf and going on holidays, Joseph.' He had never played a round of golf in his life, and holidays...well, holidays were things that were snatched in between his frantically busy life. He had always liked it that way. In fact, the last time he had been persuaded to have a week off had been six months previously when he and Isobel, at her instigation,

43

had gone to the Seychelles. After two days, he had been itching to get back into the thick of things. Did that make him a workaholic? He supposed so.

Joseph made an unconvincing sound under his breath and then added, narrowing his eyes, 'And you won't *bully* her, will you?'

He had made her sound like a scared rabbit, Bruno now thought, watching her as she gesticulated to someone he couldn't see. Her curly brown hair had been pulled back into a ponytail. From where he was standing, dressed in her shapeless, dowdy clothes, she looked more like a sparrow than a rabbit.

With a forceful stride, he walked out of the sitting room, through the kitchen and towards the outbuilding where he was surprised to hear her speaking confidently, laughing even, with the workmen, although when he coughed politely from behind her and she spun around the usual expression of wariness settled over her face like a mask.

'You're back.'

'And you sound thrilled,' Bruno drawled, taking up position next to her so that he could see what was going on. 'As thrilled as someone who's lost ten pounds and found five pence. You'd better fill me in on what's going on.' He walked restively away from her and, after a few seconds of indecisive hovering, Katy followed him and began pointing out the various areas in which progress had been made. She had not exactly obeyed his instructions about laying down laws and making demands. In fact, she had been shyly hesitant when she had visited the sprawling outdoor furniture shop in the outskirts of the city, frowning at the list of negatives that had been presented to her when she had explained the state of utter deterioration of the pool in question, tentatively explaining that money would be no object if only they could finish the job in time for when Joseph returned home.

In fact, she had found herself spending rather too much time talking about her employer, the suddenness of his heart attack and the necessity for the pool to be up and running so that he could begin his routine of gentle exercises in it. When her eyes had filled up, the kindly middle-aged man had produced a box of tissues from under the counter, and then everything had seemed to be all right.

Bruno would have had a fit if he had been a fly on the wall at the time. Katy breathed a heartfelt sigh of relief that he had been safely away in London.

The five workmen, who ranged in ages from twenty something to fifty something, had stopped what they had been doing and were deferentially pointing out the technicalities of their mission. As they spoke Bruno conducted a silent survey of the area, occasionally nodding at something that was said, asking the minimum of questions but with all evidence of being an expert on the subject and therefore incapable of being taken for a ride.

Katy could only admire it. From a distance, all that formidable self-assurance was impressive. It was only when you got close that you saw how scary it could be.

He made his careful rounds of the pool area, ending up back at the door, and she reluctantly joined him there while he instructed the men to carry on, tacking on that he assumed they would be working flat out in view of the time constraints on the job.

'Well,' he said as they walked back into the kitchen, 'all that seems very satisfactory.' He divested himself of his jacket, tossing it casually onto one of the chairs by the pine table, and turned to look at her. Her hair was a bird's nest with stray tendrils flying every which way and, having disposed of her wellingtons by the kitchen door, she had replaced these with some comfortable loafers. Thank heavens this secretarial stint would be taking place within the comfortable confines of the house because there was no way he would ever have approved a member of his own office staff turning up for work in the sort of shapeless mess that she was now wearing. In fact, that she *always* wore.

'Thank you. I...I wasn't sure that the job could be done in the time limits...but...'

'Didn't I tell you that it pays to be forceful?' Bruno nodded with satisfaction.

'You did,' Katy agreed, thinking of her considerably less than forceful approach to Mr Hawkins, the owner of the building company. 'Would you like some coffee? Tea?' It was after six. Maybe he would want something stronger. 'Or something else?' she said helpfully. 'I think there's some alcohol stashed away on one of the shelves in the larder, and there's some wine in the fridge. I think.'

'A cup of coffee would be fine.'

'Maggie's made a pie,' Katy volunteered, while she busied herself with the coffee. 'Chicken. I could heat it up for you if you like. And there's vegetables as well. She did offer to stay and dish out the supper but I told her that it was all right for her to leave. Is that okay?' She glanced at the man, now sitting in one of the chairs, which he had turned at an angle so that he could follow her movements as she spoke to him.

'I don't normally eat at six-thirty,' Bruno informed her with heavy sarcasm. 'In fact, I'm usually still at work at this time.'

'Oh. Right. Of course you are.' Katy laughed nervously. 'Joseph and I usually eat early. And before that, I used to have my supper with the children.' She slid his mug over to him and retreated to a chair at the other side of the table. 'My body clock doesn't run on a very sophisticated timetable, I suppose.'

Bruno felt torn between getting down to the business at hand, namely Joseph and what sort of routine she thought he might have when he returned from hospital, and taking her up on her throwaway remark about her eating schedules. With her fresh face and unruly hair and gauche mannerisms, she certainly looked more like a teenager than an adult, but, heck, the girl was nearly twenty-four! How many women of twenty-four would be content to be cooped up in a house caretaking an elderly gentleman, however charming the elderly gentleman was?

'And it's never bothered you,' he was slightly irritated to hear himself saying.

'What?' Katy raised her head from where she had been observing the swirling surface of her coffee and looked at him, startled.

'This.' Bruno waved one hand vaguely to encompass the house. 'Being here with Joseph. Having dinner at six-thirty. The quiet life.' He elegantly sipped from his cup as he lounged back in the chair, his long legs extended in front of him.

Katy blushed, hearing implicit criticism in his voice and not quite knowing what to do with it.

'Why should it?' she eventually said. She met his penetrating black eyes and shivered slightly. 'I'm not much of a party person, although,' she added hastily, 'I *do* go out, naturally. On my day off, I meet a couple of friends I've made in the town. Teachers. I met them at a talk in the library a few months ago.'

Bruno's ears pricked up and he idly speculated on the

possibility of the little sparrow looking at him having a raunchy double life. 'Men friends?'

Katy's face went a deeper shade of red. 'I don't really think that's any of your business,' she mumbled, mortifyingly aware that his taut, dark features had now relaxed into an expression of amusement.

'You're right. It's not,' he said, without the slightest trace of apology in his voice. 'I went to visit Joseph before I came here.' He changed the subject even though he continued watching her, reluctantly fascinated by the utter transparency of her face. That she had led a sheltered life would have been obvious to any fool at a glance. The whole world of feminine wiles appeared to have passed her by completely. He thought of Isobel with her cool, sophisticated, glamorous beauty and wondered what the two women would have made of one another.

'He's doing well, isn't he?' Katy said eagerly, her face animated as she thought back to her own visit earlier that afternoon. 'The doctors and nurses are thrilled with his progress.'

'He seems marginally less thrilled with the food,' Bruno drawled.

'He's a devil.' Katy laughed, a sweet, soft laugh that reached every bit of her face. 'I hope he wasn't trying to launch an attack on your susceptibilities because he knows very well that rich food is a no-no. I've already made that perfectly clear.'

Bruno chuckled and shot her a wicked grin. 'I think that's precisely what he was trying to do. Bland, healthy food and a swimming pool. I can see Joseph embracing this new-found life philosophy with all the gusto at his disposal.' Their eyes met in a moment of mutual amusement and then Katy blinked and looked away in sudden, inexplicable confusion.

He really was, she thought shakily, a stunningly beautiful man with just that edge of danger that would send a thrill through any normal woman's veins. She endeavoured to think of him as vividly tempting fruit that concealed some deadly poison. It wasn't really that difficult. Not then, as the moment of shared amusement was lost, and not the following day when, at eight-thirty promptly, she made her way down to Joseph's office to find him already installed, shirt sleeves rolled to the elbows, in front of his laptop computer.

He spared her a fleeting glance and, when she continued to hover by the door, impatiently told her to come inside and to shut the door behind her.

He was the archetypal employer of her worst imaginings. Having given her ten minutes to settle down in front of Joseph's computer and be brought up to date with what would be expected, he then proceeded to launch into a high-powered delivery of instructions.

Report number one was a lengthy and complex letter involving a multimillion-pound deal, which involved words that Katy had never heard before in her entire life, never mind typed.

When she finally exhaled a sigh of pure despair, Bruno shot around to where she was sitting hunched in front of the computer and proceeded to lean over her, stretching across so that he could guide the arrow down the letter, which was depressingly awash with mistakes.

'I thought you said you could type,' he said heavily, moving to sit on the edge of the desk and frown down at her.

'I warned you that this was a bad idea,' Katy muttered, her face burning. 'I'm really trying but you just dictate too fast. How am I supposed to keep up with you?'

'This is full of spelling mistakes.'

'I know!' Katy acknowledged miserably, all her dislike rising back up to the surface and making her squirm. 'I've never heard of half these words! It's all legal speak! Your secretary is probably a whiz when it comes to typing this jargon because she's accustomed to it, but I'm not! Joseph doesn't dictate business documents, he dictates *normal stuff*.' She could hear a distinct wobble in her voice and had an uncharacteristic urge to fling his laptop at his head.

'You'll have to correct it. And if it's any help you can use one of those legal dictionaries on the shelf.' He pushed himself off the desk, giving her time to gather her senses and fetch the dictionary from the shelf, knowing that she was under frowning scrutiny.

But at least for the next half an hour he wasn't breathing down her neck like a tyrant faced with an unsatisfactory serf. He relaxed back in the leather chair, which nicely accommodated Joseph and which he seemed to dwarf with his immensely powerful body, and began a series of phone calls, which Katy half listened to as she began correcting the hateful document.

If she had been a temp, she had no doubt that by the end of the day she would have had to endure a 'Your Services are No Longer Required' speech from him.

By the time she had finished the wretched thing, she realised that he was still on the phone and was unreasonably surprised to realise that this phone call was not the same as the others. He had swivelled the chair away from her and was speaking in a low, husky voice. A low, husky and very intimate voice.

She stared hard at the back of his head and was still staring when he swung the chair around to replace the receiver.

'Finished?' he asked silkily and Katy nodded and looked away.

'If you'd like some privacy to make personal calls, I really don't mind leaving...' she burst out and then blushed at the unwitting gaffe.

'What makes you think that I was making a personal call?' Bruno asked. He tilted his head back and surveyed her broodingly.

'It's none of my business,' Katy mumbled, unable to tear her eyes away.

Bruno didn't say anything. He just appeared to give her answer some consideration, then he shrugged as though coming to a decision.

'It might be.' He stood up and strolled over to the window where he proceeded to perch against the window ledge, all the better to observe her. 'And you were right. I *was* making a personal call. Nothing for which I need particular privacy, I assure you.'

'Oh. Right.' That in itself was confusing. If *she* had been making a personal call, to a man, and she assumed his had been to a woman, then she would have wanted as much privacy as she could get. Who liked their little words of endearment being overheard by all and sundry? But then Bruno was not a normal man. Maybe he just didn't do words of endearment.

'Does Joseph ever talk about my—how shall I phrase this?—my *private* life?'

'Not really, no,' Katy said evasively. The sunlight streamed from behind him so that he was starkly silhouetted. He had shoved his hands into his trouser pockets and his feet were crossed at the ankles so that his body looked whipcord lean and his shoulders broad and muscular.

'What does "not really" mean? Does it mean yes or no?'

'He's mentioned once or twice that you...that you're very popular with the ladies.'

The phrasing of that seemed to afford him a great deal of mirth and he raised his eyebrows expressively at her. 'By which I take it he thinks I sleep around?'

'That's not what he says!'

'No, but it's what he thinks. And it's also something of which he disapproves. No good denying it. But...' Bruno strung the word out until Katy was almost prompted to ask him to hurry up and finish his sentence '...he might be in for a rather pleasant surprise when he comes back. I've never brought any of the women I've gone out with back to this house before to meet Joseph.'

'I know,' Katy said involuntarily and then checked herself.

'Even though I know that what Joseph has wanted for a long time now is for me to get serious enough about a woman to invite her back here.' Bruno thought of the countless times his godfather had asked gently probing questions about his love life, tiptoeing around flatly stating that he wanted his godson to settle down, but giving off all the right vibes for the message to be conveyed nevertheless.

'And I think,' Bruno mused thoughtfully, 'that perhaps the time has arrived when I can bring a woman here to meet him.'

'Any in particular?' Katy couldn't help asking with a trace of irony because there was something so deeply unromantic about the way he had arrived at voicing his intentions. If he was in love with a woman, wanted her to meet his godfather, shouldn't he be yelling it out from the rooftops instead of deliberating on it as if it was just something else in his life that made sense at a particular point in time?

Bruno looked at her sharply, without amusement, and Katy tried to feel duly chastened.

'I've been seeing someone for a few months now and it seems to me that the time may well have come for me to settle down.'

'Because Joseph has had a heart attack and you want to make him happy now that he's recovering?'

'Because I'm not getting any younger and time waits for no man.' For someone who prided himself on his verbal dexterity, it was a little annoying to hear the clichés coming from his mouth. 'Anyway, Isobel will make the perfect wife.' He frowned and looked consideringly at Katy. 'He'll be thrilled.'

'I'm sure he will,' Katy agreed. She surprised herself by the depth of her curiosity. 'What is she like?'

'Tall. Blonde. An ex-model as a matter of fact. Her father owns one of the largest computer businesses in the country and he's expanding fast. Why are you wearing that expression?' Bruno asked irritably.

'She sounds…an ideal match,' Katy pronounced, for want of anything better to say. 'When will you invite her to meet Joseph?'

'As soon as he gets out of hospital. Of course, I won't mention my intentions straight away. I'll give him time to get to know her first. Too many surprises might have him hurtling back to the hospital for sanctuary. So, now that that's settled, shall we proceed?'

Just like that. One minute talking about something that should be the biggest event in his life and the next minute, in precisely the same detached voice, moving back onto work, as though the two were interchangeable.

And for some reason Katy found it even harder to concentrate for the rest of the day. She found her mind coming back time and again to the tall blonde model who seemed to have sprung up from nowhere and was about to step into the role of Bruno's wife and Joseph's daughter-in-law. Would she be quiet? Outgoing? Confident, Katy decided. Because Bruno would never be interested in a ditherer. Confident and chic and well groomed. Joseph would be pleased.

It was tempting to let something slip during the hospital visits that followed, but thankfully there was sufficient fertile ground for conversation without mentioning Bruno's private life at all.

At one point, she would have liked to have confided about her repeated disasters on the computer and her constant defeats when confronted with Bruno's rapid-fire delivery of letters, but after one week, to her amazement, she discovered that she was settling into his mode of command, for want of a better word.

She no longer jumped a mile whenever he came across to inspect what she had written and she was rapidly learning to diagnose his mood swings. Even his terseness contained various levels, barely noticeable to the untrained eye but glaringly obvious to the poor unfortunate who happened to be in his company for hours on end.

Except, a little voice whispered in her head as she prepared to take her leave from the hospital precisely eight days after she had started working for Bruno, she no longer considered herself an unfortunate, did she?

In fact, she was guiltily aware that the dinners they shared together had become something of a high point in her life. Then, Bruno would discuss deals with her, bouncing ideas off her as though she was a *real person* and not someone he had been compelled to use as secretarial help for want of anyone better to hand. When he asked her questions about her family, she no longer wanted to shrink inside herself because of her cursed self-consciousness.

Only the other day he had given her an odd look after she had finished a rambling monologue on some of her more depressing moments of teenage life and had said with a certain bemusement in his voice, 'You don't hold back on confiding once you start, do you?' which she had very nearly translated as a compliment until she'd realised that his face was expressing something close to curiosity in the face of something he thought might have stepped off another planet.

But at least she no longer cowered. And she actually looked him in the face when he spoke to her now instead of glancing away. He had cured her of that once and for all four days ago when he had very lightly placed one finger under her chin, tilting her head up until their eyes met, and told her that she had to lose the annoying habit of directing her conversation at inanimate bits of furniture.

And the pool was coming along in leaps and bounds, something from which she derived a lot of pleasure considering the renovations had been left totally under her jurisdiction, the results only being commented on at the end of the day when Bruno came out to have a look.

Katy found that she was humming along to something on the radio when she pulled up in front of the house to find a low-slung sports car parked at an angle in the courtyard. Against the ageing red brick of the house, it was a red, anachronistic beacon and Katy pulled the Range Rover to a stop with a hundred questions popping in her head.

They were all answered the minute she opened the front door and heard two voices coming at her from the sitting room. One she recognised and the other she had no trouble in pinpointing because it belonged to a woman and the car in the drive had smacked of glamour and money. Isobel, the mystery woman and soon-to-be wife of Bruno. Two and two, in Katy's opinion, invariably added up to four. What didn't add up was the sickening jolt she felt in the pit of her stomach as she slowly made her way towards the voices.

The door to the sitting room was flung open and she had a few seconds in which to observe the scene. Bruno was lounging against the window, a glass in one hand and smiling down at the woman who was sitting on the sofa with her back to Katy. Even from a distance of several metres apart, their bodies seemed to be leaning in to one another and Bruno was the first to pull back the minute he became aware of the figure hesitantly observing them from the door.

'You're back. Been to the hospital?'

Katy took a few steps into the room. 'Joseph wanted me to take him some library books. He's been complaining of boredom.'

'Katy, this is Isobel.'

'I…I noticed your sports car parked outside…' Katy smiled hesitantly and walked forward so that she now had a much better look at the leggy blonde on the sofa. Her pale, silky mini had ridden up her thighs, exposing what looked like impossibly long legs even in a reclining position. Her hair was an interesting blend of various shades of blonde and swung in an impressive chin-length bob around her face.

'My little run-around.' Her voice was cool and bored. 'Fab for parking in London and really quite nippy for covering long distances. So you're the secretary Bruno has working for him.' Blue eyes did a rapid inventory and were obviously satisfied at what they saw. 'He's told me all about you.'

'Oh, has he?' Katy thought of her fraught stabs at efficiency, which were frequently ambushed by her sheer lack of experience, and decided that whatever Bruno had had to say on the subject of his *secretary*, not much of it would have been flattering.

'Oh, apparently his godfather absolutely *adores* you, darling. Now why don't you come and sit next to me and we can have a nice girlie chat? Bruno, darling, why don't you fetch Kate—?'

'Katy.'

'Of course. Why don't you fetch *Katy* something to drink? We've brought some booze up with us. Bruno said that the drinks cabinet was rather depleted. I don't know how you cope without a glass or two of wine in the evenings! Clever little thing.'

Katy tentatively sat on the sofa next to the blonde. She felt as though she had suddenly been hurled into some kind of bizarre movie in which she was forced to communicate with an alien being who had mastered a form of English with which she was not familiar, and the sensation persisted for the remainder of what proved to be a very uncomfortable evening.

At least for her. Isobel was very relaxed and jarringly possessive with Bruno. Lots of casual touching on the arm, on the thigh, lots of little secret glances at him and lots of anecdotes that were intended to reveal what a beautifully suited couple they were. Bruno, uncharacteristically taciturn, seemed to view the proceedings with a mixture of assessment and amusement, which Katy found unnerving.

Maggie had cooked a splendid meal for the three of them and while Katy scurried around, setting the formal dining table because the kitchen table seemed a little too cordial for someone with such a perfect cut-glass accent, her mind did unsettling somersaults. She wondered what the two of them were doing in the sitting room. Then she laughed at herself for even bothering to think about that. Then she analysed what they had spoken about and arrived at the dismal conclusion that, next to Isobel, she had appeared even more gauche and unsophisticated than she usually was. A little brown moth alongside a sparkling butterfly. Her comfy garb seemed screamingly spinsterish in comparison with Isobel's rampantly provocative dress.

By the end of the evening, she gloomily began to understand why Bruno had showed such surprise at her chosen lifestyle. Compared to Isobel, he must have thought of her as something that had stepped out from under a stone.

The only thing that surprised her was that he insisted on Isobel driving back to London. A little blessing as far as Katy was concerned because she couldn't imagine drifting down in the morning and having to endure further feelings of inadequacy by the towering beauty.

Work, he explained, and then softened what was obviously a blow to her by reminding her what a distraction she could be.

Katy wondered, for the first time in her life, what it would feel like to be described by a man as *a distraction*. There was something so frivolous and sexy about the noun, especially when Bruno said it, with that brooding glint in his eyes.

She was dashing the last of the cutlery into the dishwasher when he strode into the kitchen and she looked up, dishevelled, to find him staring down at her.

'You don't have to do that.' He frowned. 'Maggie

would have cleared things up in the morning.' He walked into the kitchen, sat down and relaxed into the chair.

'Oh, it's no problem,' Katy said, switching on the machine and standing up. 'It's silly to leave all that stuff dirty overnight. Just makes it more difficult to clean in the morning.' And it would never have occurred to her that Isobel might lift a finger to help because fingers that well manicured did not do dishes.

She could feel her face reddening as she imagined what he must be seeing when he looked at her now.

'You're not paid to wash up,' he said irritably. 'You're not a housekeeper.'

'If the job's there to be done, then I'll do it.' Considering he had just finished spending an evening with the woman he wanted to marry, he seemed to be in a very bad mood. 'Do you still…need me around? I'm quite tired…'

'It's not yet nine! How on earth can you possibly be tired? Isn't that taking the quiet life a bit too far?'

'There's no need to lose your temper with me,' Katy told him as a little stream of anger began to swell and grow bigger inside her. 'If you're upset because Isobel went back to London, then that's not my fault! She could have stayed here overnight. It's not as though Joseph is around to be offended. In fact, I'm sure that Joseph *wouldn't* have been offended anyway.'

'Don't be ridiculous. Of course I'm not *upset* because Isobel is on her way back to London. Why on earth should I be? In case you'd forgotten, *I* was the one who suggested she leave! Tomorrow's going to be a busy day. No point having her up here, getting bored and expecting to be entertained.'

Katy's appalled reaction to this must have shown on

her face because Bruno gave her a dark frown and his mouth tightened.

'You appear to be struggling with something. What is it? Get if off your chest instead of just standing there and gaping.'

'Well…that's not a very *nice* thing to say, is it? About the woman you love and intend to marry?' Katy wondered whether her lack of experience had made her impossibly romantic and out of step with what was going on in the real world. 'I mean, shouldn't you *want* to spend time with your fiancée? I'm sure you could afford to take a day off…'

'She's not my fiancée.'

'But I thought you said…'

'I said that it was maybe time I settled down and got married. I'm thirty-four years old and playing the field becomes sad after a certain age. Isobel would make an ideal wife for me, which isn't to say that I've spoken to her about it.'

'Oh.'

Right at this moment, the expressiveness of her face was getting on his nerves because he could read exactly what she was thinking and he didn't like it. What was so wrong about being objective about the institution of marriage? He had endured his mother's headlong rush into wedlock with his two stepfathers, both of which had ended in tears. It made perfect sense to him that a lifelong union should be controlled, should be grounded in reality, should make sense on paper at least, and Isobel made sense on paper, that was for sure. She fulfilled all the necessary criteria and he had opened his mouth to coolly explain the logic when Katy said with an irksome trace of pity in her voice, 'But what about love? Romance? Magic?'

'We're not talking about someone I haven't seen, for God's sake! I won't be lifting the veil to discover that I've tied the knot with Medusa! Perhaps you're adopting this viewpoint because you didn't like her...'

Katy was uncomfortably aware that his remark had caught her by surprise and she flushed. 'That's not true!' The silence that greeted this stretched on until she stammered, 'She seemed very...very...'

'Yes? I can't wait to hear what comes next...'

'Very *elegant*,' Katy stressed positively. 'Very *sophisticated*. And, of course, she's very *beautiful* and very, very *polished*.' Katy realised that she had managed to make her sound like a piece of expensive display china.

'Elegant, sophisticated, beautiful, polished.' Bruno enumerated the virtues on his fingers. 'Yet somehow not quite the right qualities for a wife?'

'I never said that and, anyway, what I think doesn't count.'

Bruno stood up and glanced at his watch. The conversation was over because her opinion didn't count. She could read that clearly in the dismissive expression on his face.

'I have an important conference call at nine tomorrow. I'll want you to transcribe a lot of letters for me and you'll have to speed up a bit if we're to clear the lot by five. In fact, we might have to return to work after we've been to see Joseph. You hadn't anything planned, had you?'

'No.' Katy wished she had. Isobel might be a mannequin but she would bet her life that the blonde didn't sit at home reading books and watching television six nights out of seven. This quiet life was beginning to spring a lot of leaks. She couldn't wait for Joseph to be back home and for Bruno to be gone and for life to get back to what it had been.

CHAPTER FOUR

'Not bad.' Bruno pushed himself away from the desk and shot her a look that Katy could only interpret as one of mild surprise. 'Not a single spelling error. Didn't I tell you that you could do it?'

'It's nearly quarter to eight.' Katy tried not to yawn. Or move, for that matter. Her body felt as though it had been welded to the chair. Any sudden movement might result in severe physical pain. 'I've had a lot of time to correct my spelling mistakes.'

'That's the wrong attitude. You're improving. And don't run yourself down—you're a quick learner!'

Katy bit back the retort rising to her lips. They had worked until after seven-thirty for the past four days, breaking only to go and visit Joseph. Her relaxed days when she and Joseph would take their walks and amble through his memoirs now seemed like a distant memory. This cosy den, once a blissful retreat with its shelves of books and comfortable chairs, was now a high-tech office where any loitering on a comfy chair was out of the question and even breaking off to go to the bathroom was seen as an unwelcome intrusion into Bruno's ferociously high-powered routine.

'Are we finished for the evening?' She looked wistfully beyond Bruno through the window, which offered a tantalising glimpse of late spring sunshine pouring down on green trees and casting shadows across the lawns.

Bruno greeted this remark with a slight frown. 'You're

not *tired*, are you?' he demanded, looking at her narrowly so that the possibility of actually complaining went into immediate retreat. 'As I explained to you, this is a particularly important deal here and we're a little behind because of my going to London yesterday morning. Maybe next time I travel down to London, you should come with me,' he mused to himself. 'Sit in on the meeting and take notes first hand so that I don't have to transcribe them for you myself afterwards.'

'No! No, no, no.' Katy looked at him with alarm. 'I'm not your secretary...'

'You're in here working with me, you're downloading information, taking dictation, fielding calls and typing up my documents...excuse me if I got a little carried away thinking that those did in fact constitute secretarial duties...'

'*Acting* secretary,' Katy stressed, testing one foot, which seemed to be okay, no serious cramping, and then the other, '*temporarily* helping you out. Because of *extraordinary circumstances*. I couldn't possibly go to London with you and sit in on any meetings and I'm not going to!'

Bruno was highly amused to see that her normally shy countenance had tightened into determined stubbornness. Amused, but not as surprised as he might have been a fortnight ago, because working with her had shown him one thing very clearly. The painfully cowering girl who had always managed to irritate the hell out of him in the past was not quite as painfully cowering as he had expected. In fact, lurking beneath that transparent face was a streak of mulish stubbornness that was impossible to dislodge once in place. Like now. He held his hands up in mock surrender and shot her a crooked smile.

'Whoa! It was just a thought...'

'A rotten thought.' Her head filled with the nightmarish vision of sitting in on meetings with Bruno. High-powered meetings between high-powered people while she frantically tried to amass her improved but still below-par skills in an effort to take notes. She shuddered in horror at the thought. Bruno might have been accommodating to some extent in the little vacuum of Joseph's office where he was stuck with her, but she doubted he would show the slightest sympathy when in his own territory. She might have learned to cope with his presence without becoming a nervous wreck in the process but she wasn't stupid. He was still a fairly terrifying individual. She had listened in on sufficient telephone conversations to know that. When he spoke in that clipped, icily dismissive manner to someone at the other end of the line, it was all she could do not to offer up an immediate prayer of thanks that she wasn't the person being addressed.

'That's what you said two weeks ago at the prospect of working with me. It's also what you thought when I gave you the go-ahead to sort out the swimming pool area.' His dark eyes rested thoughtfully on her but there was a slight smile on his lips, the smile of someone who had proven a point. 'Anyway—' Bruno stood up, raked his fingers through his hair and moved towards the bay window where he perched on the sill and looked at her '—enough of this. It's late. I think we can call it a day for the time being.'

'I can finish those last few letters, if you like,' Katy said, guiltily aware that he could carry on for hours and was now being forced to halt in mid-stream because she was tired and hungry and her eyes were aching from staring at a computer screen.

'No. I'm nothing if not a fair employer!'

Katy shot him a sceptical look that prompted one of exaggerated mock hurt right back from him.

'Think about it, we *did* break off for a couple of hours to go and visit Joseph, so you really haven't worked overtime at all. And besides, haven't I spared you the boredom of wandering around this house with nothing to do?'

'I *do* have stuff to do, actually.'

'What?'

The stubborn expression was back on her face and her eyes slid downwards. She gave a little shrug. This, Bruno had discovered, was one of her more annoying habits. Whenever he asked her a question, usually of a personal nature, to which she did not want to reply, she gave one of those little shrugs and then looked away with a distant expression on her face that encouraged a niggle of curiosity that really got on his nerves.

Now, he ignored that and announced, 'Are you hungry? You must be. Your stomach's been making "Feed Me" noises for the past half an hour.'

Katy raised her eyes to his in mortification and automatically pressed her hand to her growling stomach. 'That...that's a very ungentlemanly thing of you to say!'

'It's the truth. Run along and get dressed. I'm going to take you out to dinner.'

'I beg your pardon?'

'You heard me. Dinner. Out. Me. You. Now hurry up. You probably want to have a bath and get into your finery.'

'We can't go out! Maggie's cooked something.'

'It'll keep. Joseph's back day after tomorrow and we need to have a little chat about what happens when he returns.'

'A little chat?' Katy had half risen from her chair and her eyes were as wide as saucers as she looked at the darkly handsome man staring back at her with thinly veiled impatience.

Yes, she had got used to working with him. In a manner of speaking. Yes, she had become accustomed to their daily drive into the town centre to visit Joseph. She could just about manage both without her nervous system going into knots. In the office, here, she kept her head down, obeyed instructions and discussed work-related matters, as she did over the dinners they occasionally shared in the kitchen. And on the drive to the hospital, they always talked about Joseph because their minds were already geared at the thought of seeing him. But *dinner* out? In a restaurant? She dredged her mind to think of a possible way out.

'That's right. Now, I'm going to finish off here and I'll see you back downstairs at…let's say…eight-fifteen? Long enough for you to get ready?' He strolled over to the desk and began leafing through some of the documents on his desk while Katy backed towards the door, finally clearing her throat to commandeer his attention.

'Yes?' Black eyes focused reluctantly on her face. 'Something else?'

'No. Oh, no. I just thought that it would be just as handy for us to eat here and discuss…well, whatever it is you want to discuss…'

Bruno frowned and gave her his full attention. 'Are you telling me that you don't want to accept my dinner invitation?' he asked flatly.

'Of course not! I just don't want you to feel…to feel that…*you have to*…'

'Why would I feel that?'

'Sort of a duty gesture, so to speak, because I've worked for you here…?'

'You're beginning to try my patience, Katy. I hadn't

really thought about it along those lines, but, as gestures go, what's wrong with this one? The arrangement has worked much better than I anticipated and, believe it or not, it *is* in my nature to reward good work.'

'Right! That's just…fine. Just wanted to make sure.' She flashed him a brilliant smile. 'Eight-fifteen?'

'If you press any harder against that door, you might just go through it.'

The gleam of his amused smile followed her while she had her bath and got dressed. She looked helplessly at her reflection in the mirror, towel wrapped tightly around her body, and then even more helplessly at the array of clothes hanging in her wardrobe. Whenever she thought of that little patronising smile in the face of her gaucheness, she had a pressing urge to startle him out of it by doing something wildly out of character. She might very well have dressed in something daring, if she possessed any such item, but a quick scan of the clothes hanging in her closet was enough to tell her that that particular shock tactic was not going to be possible.

And anyway, she reflected, once she was safely established in her flowing, calf-length dress and neat blue cardigan, which would be all she would need because it was still very mild outside despite the hour, skimpy, eye-catching clothes might seem great in her head, but in reality she would never be able to carry off the look.

The few times she had dressed in little numbers she had felt horribly uncomfortable, and her last boyfriend had kindly advised her to stay away from the vampish clothes. She had an angelic face, he had told her, and there was no point spoiling the look by trying to dress like someone from a red-light district. Katy had been pleased with the angelic look bit, though she personally couldn't see that, but vaguely annoyed at the implication that sexy was never going to be within her reach. Since when were angels interesting? The image of Isobel rose up in her head and she nearly stumbled as she made her way down the stairs.

Of course, Bruno was nowhere in evidence, and she finally unearthed him in the swimming-pool room where he was making a last-minute inspection. He barely glanced at her when she coughed to let him know that she was ready, and when he did turn to face her, inspection completed, there were no flattering phrases at the ready, not even those of the false variety.

But *he* had changed and for a split second Katy almost felt as though the breath had been knocked out of her. He was wearing black. Black jeans, black long-sleeved jumper that hung over the waistband of his trousers, black jacket casually slung over one shoulder. He looked like a dangerously well-bred highwayman and as he walked towards her she could almost feel her heart begin to crash against her ribcage.

What was wrong with her? Appalled at her own frightening regression into adolescence, she leapt into nervous chatter and the swimming pool was the easiest topic at hand. It took her through the next twenty minutes while she got herself together, although, in the car, she didn't dare let her eyes slip to the man driving.

'So what would you like to eat?' he asked, when that particular topic had been exhausted.

'Anything. I'm not fussy.'

'Makes a change to find a woman who is not fussy when it comes to food.' Bruno smiled and continued concentrating on the road. 'I have had a look at Joseph's *Where to Eat* guide and there is a good Italian a few blocks down from the hospital. That do?'

'Yummy. I love Italian food.'

'Of course, you may have been there already,' Bruno said casually and Katy glanced at him.

'What makes you think that?' She couldn't actually remember having any conversations with him along the lines of restaurants she had been to.

'Well, you mentioned that you went out for meals occasionally and there aren't exactly a riot of eating places in the town...'

'Oh, I've just really been to the pizza places. It's the quickest thing to grab if we go to the cinema. Goodness, is that the restaurant? I never even knew there was such a place around here.' They had pulled up in front of an ivy-clad house fronted by a very small courtyard, which was already almost full. Aside from the discreet sign outside announcing its purpose, it looked for all the world like someone's very tasteful private residence. Katy immediately felt self-conscious about what she was wearing and glanced down worriedly at the floral dress.

'The dress code is casual,' he said gently and Katy flushed. 'I'm not exactly dressed to kill, am I?'

'I know, but you still manage to look magnificent,' she blurted out and then wished desperately, in the growing silence, that the bottom of the car would open and swallow her up. 'I mean striking,' she amended hastily, finishing, ever more lamely, with, 'It's your colouring. I guess you could wear anything and look...well...'

'Magnificent?' He gave a low laugh that sent her blood rushing wildly through her and their eyes met, tangled and then he was opening his door and stepping out, leaving her to wallow in the embarrassment of having said precisely what she was thinking without bothering to consider the after-effects. Which appeared to be him laughing at her. Highly amused. Yet again. She miserably contemplated the status of mascot as opposed to seductress, which really was the crushing difference between her and his fiancée to be, wasn't it?

The restaurant was small and intimate and full. They were invited to wait for a table in the small snug off the dining area where coffee was taken and, once seated, Katy was subjected to one of those contemplative stares that Bruno seemed to specialise in.

'What?' she asked, going red. 'What is it? Why are you staring at me like that? It's rude.'

'Rude for a man to stare at a woman? Interesting take on things. Why is it rude?'

'Because…' Katy floundered.

'Surely you must have been stared at before? By your boyfriends? Caught up in the throes of lust?'

She sought refuge in the menu in front of her and breathed a sigh of relief when the unnerving line of conversation was dropped and he began chatting about the renovations to the pool. Not that there was much left to chat about on the subject, but she was grateful for the reprieve.

Actually, the pool was finished, all bar one or two superficial touches. Bruno had been absolutely right on that. He had given her a free hand to fling money at the project, with speed being the urgent criterion, and the workforce had risen admirably to the task. When they left the house, it was to a changed complex. Roughened, non-slip black and white tiles surrounding the actual pool had been installed in record time and the pool, which had by no means been as decrepit as first imagined, had been spruced up to the highest standard and now gleamed invitingly turquoise, ready for Joseph's first light exercise foray. She had managed to find three comfortable wicker chairs, which she had put around a low, circular table, and in the morning she might ask for time off to buy a few plants, which would thrill Joseph, maybe even convince him to linger awhile.

'I think we should reveal it to him as a wonderful surprise, no hints whatsoever that we think he might not exactly warm to the concept of actually using the damn thing as much as we want him to. And, of course, you'll have to go in with him. He cannot possibly be expected to swim lengths alone. You have a swimsuit, don't you?'

'Of course I haven't got a swimsuit, Bruno! At least, not here. Why should I?'

'Then you'll have to go out and buy one, the sooner the better.'

Katy lapsed into silence and contemplated the prospect of frolicking in a pool. She had never been a keen swimmer, something she put down to having to parade as a self-conscious fourteen-year-old in swimsuits that had always seemed to make her look even skinnier than usual. She could remember one term of obligatory swimming lessons when her lack of curves had made her cringe with embarrassment at joining in a mixed class, where the boys would ogle the girls and the girls would coyly parade their figures. At least Joseph wouldn't notice her lack of shapeliness.

She surfaced from her reverie to realise that Bruno had moved on and was now talking about something else entirely. Isobel.

'Sorry?' she said, cutting him off in mid-sentence. 'Could you repeat all that? I wasn't listening.' She smiled apologetically. 'I was daydreaming, actually,' she confided sheepishly. 'I've always had a bit of a problem with that. It used to drive the teachers crazy. They'd be talking about something, some Maths equation, and I would really start off paying attention but then I'd find my mind wandering and...'

Bruno held up one hand and gave her a long-suffering look. 'No need to go into all the details. You weren't listening. Enough said. And when, if you don't mind me asking, did your concentration begin to lapse? Funny, I've never had that effect on women before.'

'What effect?'

'Sending them asleep.'

'I wasn't asleep!' Katy protested. 'I *told* you, I was—'

'Okay, okay. I get the general picture. Well, to re-cap…' He put a lot of heavy emphasis on the word, leaving her in little doubt that repeating himself to a woman who hadn't been paying attention to him was not something he relished, 'I was talking about Isobel. Joseph is back on Saturday and I think it might be an idea if he gets to meet her on the Sunday. I can ask her up for the day, give them an opportunity to get to know one another. Why,' he sighed, 'are you frowning?'

'Was I? Oh, goodness! No. I mean, yes. Terrific idea.' Katy tried to picture Joseph's reaction to the statuesque, intimidating blonde and found that she couldn't. She also, disturbingly, found that *she* didn't much care for the thought of Isobel making another appearance, which was silly.

'Oh, yes. I can see "Terrific Idea" stamped all over your face. Spit it out, Katy. What's the problem here? You may not have liked Isobel, but I assure you that my godfather will be over the moon at the prospect of his godson finally settling down.'

'I'm sure…it's just that, well… Joseph is a bit of an old romantic at heart. Funny considering he never married.'

'Probably *because* he never married.'

Katy wondered how anyone who was so sceptical on the concept of marriage could actually be contemplating it himself, then she recalled the scrupulous list of plus points he had ticked off for her benefit in favour of the ex-model heiress and realised that marriage, for him, was probably quite different from anyone else's concept of it. Certainly very different from his godfather's who, in his strolls down memory lane, had displayed a touching faith in the power of love.

'The thing *is*...' she felt the need to expound in an anxious voice, 'you'll have to behave a little differently with Isobel when she comes, or else Joseph might just think that you're throwing yourself into something purely for his benefit. He's pretty sharp, actually.'

'I don't get it. What are you saying? No, I can sense a very long-winded explanation in the making, so let's leave it until we've ordered, shall we?'

Katy watched him as he consulted his menu with an expression that spoke volumes. Before, when he used to visit Joseph and she would engage in her evasion tactics, she had never noticed how darkly expressive his face could be. He had been a one-dimensional cut-out impressive solely for his looks, which had inspired a certain amount of awe, and his icy arrogance, which had filled her with quaking terror.

Now, having been in his company for a period of time, she could see that his arrogance contained a wealth of nuances. He could be unexpectedly thoughtful, patient in a driven sort of way and disconcertingly humorous. He still wasn't a comfortable man to be around but...

She caught herself drifting off and snapped back to reality, ordering the heartiest thing on the menu and aware that he was looking at her with raised eyebrows.

'I *told* you I eat a lot,' Katy informed him testily, not having to look at him to know what he was thinking.

'What mystifies me is *where* you put it. You have the

slimmest arms I've ever seen on a woman.' For a second, he caught himself wondering what the rest of her looked like without those shapeless clothes covering her up and almost laughed at his curiosity. 'Now, you were telling me...? About why you think I need to behave differently around Isobel if Joseph isn't to think that I'm spinning him fairy tales about wanting to marry her...?'

'You don't act like a man in love,' Katy told him bluntly.

'Oh, good grief, not this again!'

She drew in her breath and willed herself to carry on. 'You act the same when you're around her as...well...as though...'

'What would you have me do?' Bruno cut in sharply, leaning forward towards her so that she really had to steel herself not to automatically pull back. A few weeks ago she would have cringed at the power of his impact, which rushed over her in waves. Now, she continued to hold his gaze stubbornly. 'Make love to her in the dining room?'

'Don't be silly. Of course not.' Katy flushed, feeling her breathing quicken. 'But Joseph will look at you, the way you are with her, and he'll wonder why you're marrying a woman you don't seem to be madly in love with, then he'll put two and two together and get, well, four...or five or whatever...'

'What do you suggest?' Bruno asked with lively interest.

Katy shrugged, but this time he wasn't having it. He topped up her glass with more wine. 'And a shrug won't do by way of an answer. Tell me how you think a man who is madly in love with a woman ought to act.'

'I don't know,' she answered vaguely.

'Because you've never had a man madly in love with you?'

He wasn't going to trap her in this particular line of conversation, from which she would emerge a definite loser. 'You didn't seem to hang on her every word when she came over...'

'You mean like the way I'm hanging on your every word now?'

'Very funny,' Katy muttered. 'You just weren't all that...well, *solicitous*.'

'But I'm not madly in love with her.'

'Oh, Lord. You mustn't tell Joseph that. It'll break his heart.' Her own heart gave a warm little flutter. So he was prepared to marry a woman he wasn't in love with. What a cad! Nevertheless, it still gave her a peculiar, satisfied feeling to think that the striking Isobel hadn't managed to capture his heart. Huh. Not that it mattered one way or the other.

'And we wouldn't want that, would we?' Bruno said consideringly. 'Maybe...' He poured her some more wine, liking the way her cheeks were flushed and her eyes sparkled. She really had the most incredible eyes. 'Maybe you should give me some lessons on how I ought to behave around Isobel. Show me where I went wrong...I mean, what should a man who is madly in love be doing right now, were he to be sitting opposite the object of his desire?' Just for the hell of it, he thought, just to see how she'll react... He reached out and covered her hand with his and then turned her hand over so that he could stroke her palm very softly with his thumb.

For a few seconds, Katy was so startled that she literally froze, then hard on the heels of the freeze came a rush of heat that was so intense it made her head swim and her pulses race and sent funny, pleasurable little sensations racing to her breasts and between her legs. Made her feel weak and squirmy and...

She snatched her hand away, horribly confused.

'Wrong way?' He felt a cold emptiness where her hand had lain in his. He sat back and gave her his most quizzical look. 'Not expressive enough? Should I have caressed the cheek instead?' Shall we try that manoeuvre? he wanted to ask her. Then he mentally slapped his wrist and wondered, fleetingly, what the hell had just gone on there. A bit of nothing that had felt like a lot of something, though he couldn't for the life of him say what. Do him good to have Isobel around. Maybe he would invite her up for longer than just the one day. He obviously had a load of pent-up sexual energy that needed release.

'Stop it!' Katy's voice was uncustomarily sharp. 'It's not a game, Bruno.'

'No, it's not,' he said gruffly, a dark flush mounting his cheeks. 'I apologise if I breached your impeachable moral codes just then, but there's no need to hurl yourself into a state of panic at a bit of light-hearted, albeit misdirected, teasing.'

'I'm not in a state of panic!' she cried, then she lowered her voice, suddenly aware that they weren't on their own even though she felt as if they were, as if the rest of the diners simply didn't exist. 'But—' she didn't want to say this but she was going to '—I'm a person. I have feelings, you know. You might think it's a huge joke to pretend to treat me as some kind of practice ground for how you should behave with your fiancée, but I don't think it's funny at all.'

Bruno had never been spoken to like that in his life before. He couldn't think of a single woman he had ever known who wouldn't have joined in his bit of fun, enjoyed it even. A number would have liked him to have taken the pretence further, for heaven's sake! But Katy's face was a picture of embarrassment and he was well and truly poleaxed. He looked away but not for long. He felt as if he was in sudden thrall to the woman sitting opposite him, looking at him with a kind of glaring defiance.

'Okay. You're right. I…I'm sorry.'

It was such an obvious struggle for him to genuinely apologise for his behaviour that Katy relaxed and gave him a shy half-smile. Her body felt as if it was getting back to a state of normality too. Which was good because what she had felt when he had touched her, a meaningless touch for him, a bit of a joke, had left her shaken and scared. Scared because she had never felt such an intense sensation before. As if every nerve ending in her body had been electrified.

She was quietly relieved when their food appeared, giving them something mundane to focus on. They talked about Joseph as well, and, staying well away from any topic that could be seen as remotely controversial, Bruno talked a bit about himself, about his childhood and his boarding-school experiences, only confiding when they were drinking their coffee that she was the first woman he had bored with stories of his youth.

'They weren't boring at all,' Katy said, surprised that he could even think that. In some confusion, she thought that nothing about him was boring. 'How can you ever really know someone unless you know about their past? It's our history that makes us the people we are now, don't you think? Gosh, that's a little deep, isn't it?' She laughed awkwardly and sipped some of her coffee, which was as good as the rest of the meal had been. She had finished every morsel of her food, to his amazement, and had laughed at the expression on his face when she had finally closed her knife and fork.

'Now *my* past!' She rested her elbows on the table and cradled the cream cup between her hands, looking at him over the rim, making little notes in her head about his beautiful face, its dark contours, the length of his lashes, the way his eyes could look lazy yet alert at the same time. 'I guarantee you'd fall asleep into your coffee if I were to tell you about it.'

'Happiness is never boring,' Bruno told her. 'You had a happy childhood, two loving parents. That's why you are the way you are...' He gave her a strange look and then glanced down into his coffee, only breaking off to signal for the bill.

'Which is what...?' Three glasses of wine, not even three because there was still some left in her glass, and she felt utterly relaxed. 'No, don't tell me. I don't think I want to know.'

'Why not?' An amused smile tugged the corners of his mouth.

'Because it's bound to be critical. I know,' she carried on without rancour, 'that you don't think you are, but you're a very critical person. You can't help yourself.'

'And you are...' he paused and looked at her from under his lashes '...frighteningly honest.'

'Was that what you were going to tell me?' Katy released a sigh of relief.

'Honest and sincere and bewilderingly uncynical.'

'What have I got to be cynical about?' Katy asked, bemused by his interpretation of her personality. As though he had never met anyone who possessed those qualities before when, in fact, she would have said that they all added up to a very average and unremarkable person. But then, in his world, perhaps honesty was a rarity. He was an incredibly rich and powerful man and she knew that men like that were courted, fawned upon and surrounded mostly by people who would trip over themselves to agree with every word he said. And his adversaries probably moved around him like sharks, waiting for the moment when they could home in and make their kill.

'You're right. What *have* you got to be cynical about?' he agreed, standing up and escorting her to the door, where they were profusely thanked by the manager of the restaurant and urged to come back soon.

'Poor Bruno, I feel so sorry for you!' Katy burst out impulsively and then swiftly regretted the impulse when she saw his features tighten. When would she ever learn not to shoot her mouth off with this man? She was all right for a while, then suddenly she would say something stupid. Like now. 'Sorry,' she said quickly, edging away a bit as they walked to where he had parked the car. 'Idiotic thing to say.'

'Why do you feel sorry for me?' Out of the light, she could no longer see his expression. He sounded curious enough—politely curious, but who could tell with Bruno? Since he asked though...

'I'd hate to be surrounded by hard-nosed cynics,' she confided, pausing as he opened the car door for her and then slipping into the passenger seat. 'How do you ever know whether someone really likes you or not?' she carried on as he pulled out of the courtyard at a leisurely speed. 'You must always have to watch what you say and think about what you do...' At this juncture, she remembered Isobel, the woman he was not madly in love with but presumably deeply fond of with whom he could at least open up and be himself. Good to think about Isobel, a salutary reminder that this was not a date between a man and a woman getting to know one another. This was a 'thank you for services rendered' meal out.

'So isn't it brilliant that you have Isobel there? Someone you can be yourself with!' she finished bracingly.

Bruno gave a grunt, which Katy interpreted as agreement even though she might have expected something a little more forthcoming on the subject, and then lapsed into such concentrated silence that eventually she felt compelled to carry on.

'I feel I ought to apologise…' she began.

'Again? What for this time?'

Katy, thinking about her over-exaggerated reaction to his bit of teasing earlier on in the evening, was absently aware that his tone sounded a bit clipped, but she didn't dwell on that. She was too busy dwelling on her gaucheness when he had touched her, jumping back as though she'd been burnt and then giving a speech about not being the sort of girl who played games like that. How unbearably puerile must he think her to be? Not to mention prudish and moralistic? Just the thought of Isobel had brought the unwelcome memory rushing back at her.

'About the silly way I reacted when you were teasing me earlier on. Remember? When you held my hand and asked me to show you how a man who's madly in love with a woman should behave? Well, I guess I overreacted a bit. A lot, actually. And it was presumptuous of me to tell you how you should behave anyway!'

'So,' Bruno murmured softly, sending her a glance, 'are you telling me that you're willing to give me some lessons after all?' Naturally he knew the answer, but the thought of such a thing happening made his loins stir in immediate response, and before he could kill the thought his imagination broke free and was filling his head with all sorts of incredible images.

'Of course I'm not!' Joking again, Katy thought. But this time she wasn't going to act morally outraged. Just laugh it off as he expected.

Shame, Bruno caught himself thinking. Then he thought of Isobel. He'd get in touch with her in the morning. Invite her up for the Sunday but tell her that she might as well bring an overnight bag. A warm, willing woman in his arms was just what he needed right now.

CHAPTER FIVE

'IT'S...it's splendid.'

Joseph had been collected from the hospital in high spirits. The nurses had all found him irresistible and he had been tickled pink to find himself surrounded as he was installed in his wheelchair with Bruno and Katy right behind him. He had presented Matron with a lavish floral arrangement and several boxes of handmade Belgium chocolates and in turn they had handed over a gigantic card signed by every member of staff who had helped look after him, including his consultant.

His buoyant spirits, however, seemed to have taken something of a dive as he dubiously regarded the swimming-pool complex.

'Come and sit in one of the chairs,' Katy said, gently tugging him over to the two-seater wicker chair with its plump, squashy cushions before he could turn tail and head back into the house. 'Right now, my dear? Shouldn't I be inside, resting?'

'We thought we'd have lunch here,' Bruno said conversationally. 'Maggie's made something light.'

'How light? I suppose,' Joseph said gloomily, allowing himself to be led towards the little cluster of chairs and eased into one, 'you've been given a wretched diet sheet. A man of my advancing years shouldn't be confined to bland, unsalted, non-spicy foods for the rest of his days. What's the advantage of growing older if you find yourself having to eat macaroni and grilled fish for the rest of your life? Eh?'

'Now isn't that comfortable?' Katy said brightly, sitting next to him and still managing to see Bruno as he lowered himself into the other chair, even though she wasn't really looking in his direction.

'Not bad,' Joseph admitted. 'All that water's a little off-putting, though. I expect you'll be wanting me to get into it at some point? I'm not a very strong swimmer, you know. Never have been. I could very easily drown.'

'It's heated,' Katy elaborated, reluctantly eyeing Bruno, who had sprawled into the chair and had lazily extended his legs, letting his head rest back so that his eyes were half closed.

'And Katy will be very disappointed if you refuse to sample the water,' he drawled. 'She's been a little beaver trying to get this complex up and running before you got back. Haven't you?' His black eyes slid across to her.

'Have you, my dear?' Joseph's voice brightened. 'You shouldn't have!'

'I enjoyed it. And you will have a little dip, won't you, Joseph? The consultant says some light exercise would be very good for you. I mean, I'm not suggesting that you dash to your room for your bathing costume *this very instant*, but maybe tomorrow…?'

'*Tomorrow?* How on earth could I possibly go for a swim tomorrow when I'm going to be meeting my godson's…' he leant towards Katy and threw a sly look at Bruno who was now staring at them with a little frown '…well, not quite sure what to call her but it must be serious considering she's the first woman he's ever dared bring to the house…'

Bruno was wearing a trapped look on his face. They had both casually mentioned Isobel and her imminent arrival the next day on the way back from the hospital. Bruno had been unforthcoming virtually to the point of reticence, but that hadn't stopped Joseph from launching into a detailed interrogation, which had taken up the better part of the drive back to the house. The more detailed the questions, the more monosyllabic Bruno had become to the point where, once Joseph had been settled in the kitchen for a little chat with Maggie, who had been restlessly waiting for her employer to return, Katy had felt compelled to remind him that he was introducing his godfather to his prospective daughter-in-law.

'I'm aware of that,' Bruno informed her irritably. 'Not,' he reminded her, 'that Joseph is supposed to know that the relationship is that serious.'

'Why do you have to make it all so complicated? Why don't you just tell him that you're going to be marrying Isobel instead of dodging his questions, which is only going to make him wonder what's going on between the two of you?'

'Leave my private life to me, Katy,' was all he said and there was enough ice in his voice to make her realise that further questioning from her was not going to be tolerated.

Now Joseph was asking whether he would be required to dress up for Isobel or whether she was the sort of girl who would take him as he was.

Katy found it hard not to giggle at Joseph's transparent digging and at the way Bruno greeted the question by dropping his dark sunglasses over his eyes. She would never have imagined that this big, powerful dynamo could do something as normal as squirm but he was as close to squirming as he could get. She could almost see his shoulders sag with relief when Maggie came in to ask them whether they were ready for a bit of lunch. He vaulted out of the chair with alacrity, leaving her to chat with Joseph while he made a show of helping bring in the lunch and then, over lunch, sidestepped all chat of Isobel with the mastery of a practised escapologist.

'I'll need you back down in the office to do some work for me,' he told her, once lunch had been cleared away and Joseph had been taken up to his room for the rest he now claimed he no longer wanted.

'But it's *Saturday*,' Katy protested, frowning. 'And I know I'm not back into my normal routine with Joseph yet, but—'

'But as far as you're concerned, you're now relieved of all secretarial duties with me, am I right? Even though several things still need finishing.'

'No, of course not,' Katy said, blushing. 'It's just that I assumed…'

'Meet me in the office in half an hour and you needn't worry that I'll keep you there for the next eight hours. I just want those emails we were working on yesterday to be sent and I'll need you to write a letter after I've had my conference call.'

At which he spun around and abruptly headed off towards the office, leaving her to wonder why he was in such a ferocious mood when Joseph was now back home, as hale and hearty as could be expected, and his girlfriend was arriving the following morning.

'Doesn't seem too exuberant on the subject of this Isobel creature,' Joseph told Katy as soon as they were in his suite and she was fishing out his book for him to read. 'Not sure I like the sounds of her, anyway.'

'You can't say that, Joseph. You haven't met her as yet.' Katy decided that she'd better err on the part of reticence just in case her own lukewarm opinions began filtering through. She turned his favourite chair towards the window so that he could have a view of the sun drenched lawns outside.

'Why is he so uncommunicative about her? Must be keen to be bringing her here, so you'd have thought *I* would have been the one to have been putting a stop to his chatter!'

'You know Bruno. He doesn't "chatter".' Katy wasn't looking at him when she said this. She was tugging open the sash window so that some of the light spring breeze could waft into the bedroom. She didn't see the expression flit over his face. When he next spoke, his voice was mild, almost absent-minded.

'Very contained, yes,' Joseph said, sinking into the chair with a sigh of pleasure and reaching out for his book. 'Genuine, though, that's the thing. Glad you two got along. Now, are you going to read to me, my dear?'

'I can't. Well, I *could* but Bruno wants me to finish off some work we started yesterday…'

'In which case, you run along and don't let him overwork you.'

'Oh, I've learnt how to put my foot down.' She laughed softly and shuffled a little table next to him so that he had somewhere to rest his spectacles and his glass of water.

Bruno was waiting for her with his back to the door when she entered the office ten minutes later.

She went straight to the computer, sat down and waited for him to fire out his usual list of instructions. He didn't. In fact, he didn't turn around to face her, and eventually she said, clearing her throat, 'Are we going to get down to this work, Bruno? If we hurry, I can probably manage to take Joseph for a late stroll in the garden before dinner. I know he's dying to see how all his plants are doing. He doesn't believe me when I tell him that they've been looked after.'

'In a minute.' He turned to face her, blocking some of

the light pouring through the window, and stuck his hands into his pockets. 'Just need to have a chat about work, actually.'

'Oh, right. Have I done something wrong?' Katy frowned and tried to remember what particular typing disaster she might have managed to produce. She thought she had succeeded in a basic level of competence, but for all she knew he might have taken exception to something she had inadvertently rephrased. Hopefully, she hadn't done something really catastrophic like delete files. She avoided that particular button like the plague but...

'No need to look so chewed up,' Bruno said, pushing himself away from the window ledge and sinking into his chair, which he turned so that he could face her squarely. 'You're proving to be quite an efficient little secretary.'

'What, then?'

'I'd thought, originally, that once Joseph was back I would return to London but I'm beginning to think that I couldn't possibly leave just at the moment.'

Katy hadn't actually contemplated him leaving and was disconcerted to find that the prospect of that was not exactly the shining ray of sunshine on the horizon that she would have expected it to have been.

'Why not?'

'I shall have to wait until I'm personally satisfied that everything is fine here.' He reached out for his pen and began idly tapping it on the surface of the desk. 'Which, I'm afraid, means that you're going to have to continue working for me for a bit longer.'

'But I really should be devoting my time and attention to Joseph...'

'I'm sure he'll understand and, besides, things are going to take a little while before they return completely to normal, aren't they? He won't be running around the minute his feet hit the ground here. If anything, we'll have to work out an arrangement whereby you can spend some time here in the office…'

'Well, isn't that going to be a bit unsatisfactory?' Katy frowned, bemused. 'How are you going to get through what you have to get through if you don't have someone working for you full-time?'

'Leave me to sort that out.'

'So will there be some sort of…timetable?'

'Think out of the box, Katy.' He stood up and began prowling the room restlessly. 'There won't be a timetable.' He paused to stare down at her. 'You'll just have to be prepared to go with the flow.'

'Go with the flow?'

'Correct.'

'Are you sure that's going to work?' She was finding it hard to imagine how he could alter his pace from ferociously work propelled into a loose 'going with the flow' lack of schedule. 'If you intend to be here for a bit longer and Joseph is back, mightn't it be better for you to get someone full-time? What about Isobel? Maybe she could take over. Does she, well…would she fit the bill?'

That suggestion was ridiculous enough to make Bruno perch on the edge of his desk, all the better to display his utter incredulity at the thought.

'Isobel has never done a proper day's work in her life. In fact, work for Isobel can be summed up by the efforts she is sometimes required to take when the family chauffeur is otherwise engaged and she has to take a taxi to Knightsbridge instead to do her shopping. Work, for Isobel, is deciding what colour her nails should be painted.'

'Why are you thinking about marrying her if you disapprove so much of her lifestyle?'

'Did I imply that I disapproved of her lifestyle?' He was beginning to wonder what had possessed him to think that Isobel might be the ideal mate for him. But she was coming up and Joseph was already getting in a tizzy about the possibility of someone serious in his life. He could tell. All those questions, all that not very subtle tiptoeing around the suggestion that this might be The One.

He reminded himself that she was very eligible and very beautiful and would be a very agreeable woman to have on his arm in public.

Unfortunately, meeting Katy's cornflower-blue eyes, he was still aware that he was somehow being accused by her of something. Which was really getting on his nerves.

'She's not that unusual,' he was reluctantly compelled to expound.

'Maybe not.'

'I only hope that Joseph takes to her.' He gave Katy a brief, uncertain glance and flushed. 'Did he mention anything…?'

'No.' Katy dropped her eyes and looked hard at the keyboard of the computer. She didn't think that Joseph was going to rush headlong into full-fledged adoration of the lady in question, but not in a thousand years would she have voiced that opinion. Bruno obviously considered her the ideal mate. He might just find that he and Isobel were the only two amongst them who shared that opinion, she thought, and then caught herself for thinking such a petty thing. It was just a shame that she was coming so soon, barely giving Joseph time to gather himself.

The following morning, she revised that opinion when

she was greeted by an extremely lively Joseph, whom she helped to change into his best Sunday garb of a tweed jacket and a pair of brown trousers.

'You look good enough to have tea with the Queen,' Katy joked as they had breakfast in the kitchen. There was no sign of Bruno and she felt a little stab of sourness at the thought of him decking himself out to greet his guest. He hadn't gone out of his way the last time he had brought Isobel over, but then this was different. This time she was meeting family.

As the morning ticked past she felt more and more like a spare wheel and the effect was complete when, at ten-thirty, Bruno appeared to join them in the garden. In the clear light of early summer, he looked breathtakingly beautiful in a cream polo shirt and some beige trousers. His hair gleamed in the sunlight and she found herself staring at the classic, hard profile as though it were the first time she was seeing him.

She shouldn't really be here. She didn't belong. This was a family affair and she shrank into the background, keeping silent as Bruno and his godfather chatted, listening out for the sound of a car purring up the drive and wondering how she might be able to slink away when no one was looking.

By the time the car finally did pull up, Katy had lapsed into a complex reverie involving her imminent escape, barely aware of Bruno's frowning glances in her direction or of Joseph's watchful eyes flitting between the two of them.

'I hope you intend to be a little chattier when we go in,' Bruno muttered into her ear and Katy blinked and looked at him.

'Why?' For once she had no desire to be anything but blunt and he narrowed his brilliant dark eyes on her.

'Because it would make for a more comfortable atmosphere? Because Joseph might feel a little more relaxed if he didn't know you were there in the background, fulminating?'

'I don't fulminate,' Katy muttered back under her breath. 'In fact, I don't even know what that means.'

'Why are you sulking?'

'I wasn't sulking. I was just thinking that I'd be better off somewhere else. Then the three of you could get to know one another without me being around.'

'Stop feeling sorry for yourself. It's a very irritating trait. I thought you'd got past that.'

He left her with that thought to go and open the front door and then for a few minutes she actually succeeded in forgetting how redundant she felt as Isobel swept in, leather holdall in one hand, the other reaching up to curve around Bruno's face so that she could draw him down and plant a lingering kiss on his mouth. She was one of those women who carried about them a flurry of activity. There was nothing restful about her. Out of the corner of her eye, Katy noticed that Joseph was looking a little dazed by the six-foot blonde as she commandeered the attention and lavished her conversation on him, drawing him towards her with the proprietorial air of someone who had launched herself into a mission with one hundred and ten per cent enthusiasm. Katy wondered whether in fact Bruno had already proposed. She certainly seemed to be playing the part of intended bride with everything at her disposal.

The performance, however, did not extend to her, Katy noticed. She was resolutely relegated to the background and was quite happy to take up her position there and observe from the sidelines.

Isobel made her nervous and she didn't quite understand why. Maybe it was because she was so over-the-top in everything. Her clothes were dashing and bold; her voice reached every corner of whatever room they happened to be in; she never appeared to be short of conversation. It was quite awe-inspiring, really. Whether Joseph was responding to all this lavish attention was very hard to tell. He was, as always, perfectly polite in his usual understated, gentlemanly way, listening with his head slightly cocked to one side and showing just the right level of interest.

It was only when lunch had been served that Katy noticed a certain tiredness around his eyes and she gently suggested that it might be time for him to go upstairs and get a little rest.

'My goodness!' Isobel exclaimed, turning away from a red-faced Maggie who had found herself the object of effusive compliments on the sumptuousness of her salmon. 'Darling, I barely *remembered* that you were there! Such a silent little thing, isn't she?'

'Serene.' Joseph paused with his hand on the door and looked at Isobel. 'Calming. I have always considered those very alluring traits in a woman.' It was as close to a criticism of their guest as it was possible for Joseph to direct and it embarrassed the life out of Katy who, having retreated into observant silence, was now subjected to Isobel's resentful stare and Bruno's narrowed, inscrutable eyes.

Isobel recovered quickly. 'Oh, absolutely!' she gushed, edging very close to Bruno and nestling against him. 'Awful shame that a quiet woman is virtually an invisible woman in London, isn't it, darling?' She gazed up at Bruno, staking her claim. 'And that wouldn't do at all in the sort of life that *we* lead.' Her smile made it quite clear that she was establishing her territory and pointedly placing herself in the category of ideal wife material for the man standing by her side. Over her head, Bruno met Katy's eyes and she looked away quickly. But her heart was pounding and she was flushed at the implied put-down.

'It's very hectic in London, Joseph,' Katy said now, moving to his side. 'You need to be aggressive.' Her smile felt forced. 'And now to bed for a short nap. Shall I read to you?' She turned towards Bruno and Isobel and noticed that he had detached himself from her side and was pouring himself a glass of wine, leaving his fiancée stranded in the middle of the room. 'Joseph has solemnly promised me that a bit later he might just put one toe into that swimming pool...'

'And you're going...where...?' Bruno asked her.

'I beg your pardon?'

'I take it you're about to disappear? When Joseph is settled why don't you come down and join myself and Isobel in the pool?' Bruno was leaning against the walnut sideboard and staring at her over the rim of his glass, even when he tilted his head back so that he could swallow some of the wine. His eyes didn't leave her face. Across the width of the room, Katy felt the force of his personality rush towards her like a gust of wind and she even took a slight step backwards in confusion.

'I...thank you, but I think I'll just...'

'You *did* buy a swimsuit, didn't you?'

The stranded Isobel clearly didn't care for the tenor of the conversation, because she glided towards Bruno, who didn't appear to notice her at all.

'Yes, of course I did!' Katy flushed and looked away. Did he have to treat her like a minor? It was bad enough when they were on their own, but in the presence of his girlfriend it was unforgivable. The problem was that she lacked the necessary turn of phrase to tell him so. She was not adept at being clever with words so she bit back her mortification.

'Don't bully the poor little thing,' Isobel chided. 'And never you mind,' she addressed Katy with eyes that were as cold as chips of ice, 'if you didn't buy a swimsuit. It's not the end of the world. I've brought a couple up myself and I *would* lend you one but…' her eyes slid over Katy's slight frame, enveloped in a loose-fitting dress '…it probably wouldn't fit. We're entirely different body shapes.'

Katy was gloomily aware that there was nothing she could possibly say to refute that obvious statement. Isobel was a tall, full-breasted beauty who turned heads and could command attention. She, on the other hand, was a timid little thing with a flat chest and would not have been able to turn heads if she danced naked on a table in a crowded room. Before Joseph, full of all the right intentions, could come to her defence with some glaringly fictitious compliment, she hurriedly exited the room with as much dignity as she could muster under the circumstances.

'Odious woman,' Joseph said as soon as they were out of earshot.

'But beautiful,' Katy replied wistfully. '*Not* that I'm implying that she's odious. It's just that when you're as beautiful as that, well…it must be very easy to be dismissive of other people.' Other plain, dowdy people, she thought on a sigh, like me. She wondered what it must be like to be blessed with such staggering beauty and then decided that she was rather relieved not to know, if staggering beauty came with a vicious tongue. 'I have to stop running myself down,' she said, more to herself than to Joseph. 'According to Bruno, I do that far too much.'

'Don't know what he sees in her,' Joseph huffed, taking the stairs slowly. 'Problem with beautiful people is that they're always wrapped up in themselves.'

'Bruno's beautiful,' Katy pointed out.

'You think so, do you?'

'I mean,' she stressed, 'from a purely objective point of view. They're both beautiful. They make a very attractive couple.'

'How serious is this? Has he told you? Mentioned anything…?'

'If you're concerned, you ought to ask him yourself,' Katy suggested evasively.

'Might just do that. Now no need to spend time reading to me. Fancy a little kip anyway. Got to build my strength up if I'm to go anywhere near that pool later this evening.'

'You can sit on the side, Joseph. No one's asking you to plunge in and start swimming lengths.'

'You'll come in with me, won't you? I mean, you *did* buy that swimsuit, didn't you?' He directed a sly little smile at her, which made her laugh.

'Yes, I did!'

'Well, we'll wait until much later. When the viper's out of the pool.'

'That's very unkind, Joseph,' but she was finding it hard not to giggle at the description, which was remarkably accurate. She wondered, for a few seconds, whether proximity to water mightn't turn the glamorous Isobel into a reptile of some sort, and then chastised herself for her lack of generosity.

He *did* have a point, though. Isobel didn't strike her as an avid swimmer. She would probably enjoy lounging around the pool in a revealing swimsuit, and when that palled she would be more than happy to go indoors and have some pre-dinner drinks. And Bruno, naturally, would follow her. In that window of vacancy, she and Joseph would be able to have a relaxing half an hour there.

She waited a decent length of time, plenty long enough for Bruno and Isobel to have changed and headed to the pool, then Katy retreated to the snug with her book. Under normal circumstances, she would have spent the next two hours lost to the world. This was a particularly riveting biography. After half an hour, she realised, with surprise, that she had managed to read a page and a half and then she further realised, with a little stab of guilt, that she had spent most of the time thinking about Bruno and Isobel, wondering what they were doing. Swimming? Cavorting in the water? Doing *other things*? Surely not! Katy snapped shut the book and leaned back on the chair with her eyes closed and her imagination wide open and horribly alert.

When she heard the sound of voices and footsteps approaching, she shot out of the chair, clutching her book, as if she had been caught red-handed with her thoughts spread around her on the carpet. Before she had time to compose herself, there they were, the couple from the centre pages of a magazine. Straight from the pool. Bruno had slung on a shirt which, unbuttoned, exposed a slither of bronzed, muscled torso and Isobel was virtually unclothed. Just a wisp of a bright pink bikini top that left very little to the imagination and a light wrap-around thing that was the last word in casual elegance. Below the short hemline, her long legs seemed to go on and on for ever.

'I was just reading!' Katy blurted out. 'How was the pool? Did you have a nice swim?'

'You should have come in with us.' Bruno strolled lazily into the room and proceeded to drop into one of the chairs. 'Seemed a shame that the pool was christened without you when you were the one responsible for getting it finished.' He dangled his sunglasses idly from one hand and glanced across to Isobel. 'Why don't you go and change? It's…nearly five. You can join me for drinks in the sitting room around seven-ish. I need to do a bit of work.'

Isobel pouted. 'On a *Sunday*, Bruno?'

'The great money-making machinery never goes to sleep, Isobel. It certainly doesn't take weekends off.' He sighed and gave her his full attention. 'I'll try and keep it to a minimum.' Then that smile that could melt ice. 'In fact, why don't you go upstairs and wait for me? Hmm? I'll come up as quickly as I can…'

Not quite knowing where to look, Katy hovered in embarrassed silence, staring at the ground with her fingers curled around the book, waiting for him to leave. He didn't and eventually she risked a glance upwards to find him looking at her.

'You're doing it again,' Bruno said curtly. 'And before you ask *doing what*, you're looking like a rabbit caught in some headlights. Sit down, why don't you?'

'I thought you were going off to do some work.'

'I have an email to send. Shouldn't take longer than a few minutes.'

Katy sat down, horrendously aware of his presence, and opened the book in front of her. She was confronted by a jumble of print that didn't make much sense but she continued peering at the page anyway.

'You're going to *read*?'

'Sorry?'

'I don't expect you to sit there reading when I'm in the room,' Bruno informed her with such sweeping arrogance that she almost gasped aloud.

'Shall I go upstairs?'

'He doesn't like her.'

Cutting through the preliminaries and getting right down to the gist of the matter. Katy closed the book and met Bruno's glittering black eyes steadily.

'He doesn't like her and, furthermore, it was a ludicrous idea to bring her up here. What did he tell you and don't even bother trying to prevaricate, Katy.'

Caught on the end of a hook, Katy cleared her throat and tentatively said, 'I think he thinks that she's a little…overpowering…'

'You didn't lead him to think that marriage was on the cards, did you?'

'Of course not!' she protested stoutly. 'You told me not to say anything and I didn't.' Why? she was desperate to ask. Are you having second thoughts? Then, like a bolt of lightning that came from nowhere, she realised that that was what she was hoping. Hoping that his perfect arrangement would come to nothing because, Lord above, she had only gone and done the unthinkable, had only started seeing him as a man, and a deeply attractive one at that, instead of as a temporary employer with a heart as cold as ice.

Everything now seemed to slot together magically, like pieces of a jigsaw puzzle. The way she felt on edge, nervous, *excited* whenever she was in his company, as if he had turned a switch on inside her and brought her to life. The way she followed him with her eyes, was aware of him even when she wasn't actually looking at him, in fact was aware of him even when he wasn't in her line of vision! All those uncharitable thoughts about Isobel had their roots in good, old-fashioned jealousy.

Did she really think that he was going to dump such an ideally suitable mate as Isobel just because Joseph hadn't immediately warmed to her? He thought things through with his head and not his heart and, just in case he was thinking about asking her to try and engage in some kind of promotional campaign on Isobel's behalf to his godfather, Katy stood up with a determined expression.

'Where are you going?'

'I'm leaving you to get on with your work and, besides, it's…' she made a pointed show of looking at her watch '…time for Joseph to start getting ready for his little jaunt in the pool.' She could *feel* Bruno's fulminating silence as he continued to look at her. 'I think he's more tempted by the water than he lets on,' she rattled on, desperate now to get out of the room so that she could start processing her thoughts. 'He's made a huge show of saying how much he loathes swimming but…' she giggled nervously '…I think it's a case of all bark and no bite, don't you? Or have I used the wrong cliché?' For a few seconds she remained where she was, hovering, like a candidate at an interview, then she made her legs move in the direction of the door, almost expecting him to summon her back and dreading it because if he started dredging her thoughts, then goodness only knew what might come out.

He didn't, though, and Katy half ran up the stairs, only stopping *en route* to her room to inform Joseph that they could head down to the pool.

'Coast clear?' he whispered in a wickedly conspiratorial tone, which she ignored. 'I may be old but I'd rather not show myself up…'

I know the feeling, Katy thought fifteen minutes later as she shut the door to the swimming-pool area behind her. Luckily the house had been silent when they had come down the stairs. She discarded the towelling robe she had thrown over her swimsuit, a modest black one-piece with some cunning lacing down the front that she had tied firmly at the top.

It was not what Bruno saw when he quietly entered the room half an hour later. His godfather, apparently through with his stint in the pool, was sitting on one of the chairs looking extremely rested with his eyes shut and his book on his lap, and there she was, emerging from the water, not looking in his direction at all. Her head was lowered as she squeezed her hair with her hands. One foot rested on the side of the pool, the other was still on the step in the water.

He didn't know why he had come. Isobel was presumably waiting for him in the room that had been allocated to her, but her attractions had not been enough to get him up those stairs to see her.

He found that he was holding his breath, looking at Katy, at the body she had always kept well hidden. Long, slender legs, a slightness that bordered on gamine, breasts that pushed provocatively against the wet black Lycra with the lace that was coming undone. He couldn't drag his eyes away from her and he wasn't sure how long he would have just continued standing there and watching if she hadn't then looked up and registered his presence.

CHAPTER SIX

A SLOW, curling heat spread through Katy's body as their eyes locked. Bruno was looking at her, really looking at her and this time his expression wasn't shuttered. He dragged his eyes away from her face and then slowly appraised her frozen body with shocking intimacy, starting with her shoulders and moving right down to the tips of her toes, then back upwards, lingering on the slightness of her waist and the small roundness of her breasts. He moved forward and that snapped her out of her trance. She immediately folded her arms protectively across her breasts, trying to cover the body she had always considered too boyish to be attractive.

Her heart was beating like a hammer inside her and she almost yelped in alarm as he walked towards her and said roughly, 'Don't.'

'D-don't what…?' Katy stammered. Now that she had absorbed the initial shock of looking up and just seeing him there, intense mortification was beginning to set in. She was very modestly covered up in her one-piece swimsuit, but she felt as if she were standing in front of him in full nudity. Even worse was how her body was reacting. Her breasts were tingling and she felt as if she were melting between her legs.

Instead of answering, he carefully pulled her arms away from their fiercely folded position and dragged them down to her sides.

'Don't try and cover up your body like that,' he murmured huskily.

Katy blushed in wild confusion and glanced over her shoulder desperately.

'He's dozed off,' Bruno said, following her glance and reading what was in her head. 'That small spot of exercise must have exhausted him.' His brilliant eyes refocused on her.

'Yes, well…he's done awfully well, actually…'

'Why do you wear the clothes that you wear? Great things that cover you up?' As if he couldn't help himself, his gaze lowered to roam over the soft swell of her cleavage and the tantalising glimpse of skin visible underneath the loosely undone lacing. 'I'd never have guessed that you had a body like this…'

'Like what?' Katy whispered, then she realised, belatedly, that this was not the kind of conversation that should be taking place between them, even though there was something wonderfully thrilling about it. Bruno might be noticing her, sort of in the way that he might notice something that he had taken for granted only to find that he had inadvertently missed something, something like a table with a concealed drawer underneath, but he would be noticing her *dispassionately*. She repeated the word in her head, using it to get a grip on herself. If only the feel of his long fingers weren't scorching her skin and sending her nervous system into crazy overdrive!

'Slender. Smooth, like satin. But with curves in all the right places.'

'No. No, no, no.' Katy shook her head to block out the velvety sexiness of his voice. 'Look, I'm beginning to feel cold. I need to get my towel. And Joseph…he really should get up now or he'll be in a very bad mood when he finally does…'

'You're cold,' Bruno murmured. 'Is that why your nipples are so erect?'

Even knowing him as she now did, knowing that he was the archetypal dominant male who spoke his mind with a forthrightness that often bordered on arrogance, Katy was still unprepared for the directness of his question. Her mouth fell open in absolute, dumbfounded shock—not that he looked in the least bit repentant.

'You shouldn't be talking to me like this,' she squeaked shakily. 'You…you *have a fiancée*…'

'Which is something that's been under consideration, in point of fact. You still haven't answered my question. Is your body responding to the cold or to me?' For a man who had always prided himself on his formidable self-control, Bruno now felt himself to be in the grip of something dangerously unsettling. Without giving a passing thought to the consequences, he brushed his finger lightly over one nipple, and when he felt the bud tighten fractionally in response he almost groaned aloud. Not very cool, he thought unsteadily. Not much like the man he normally was, the one who always led the dance when it came to women and turning them on. He heard her indrawn gasp with a rush of satisfaction. Her appalled face might be frantically telling one story, but her body was busy telling another. And the story her body was telling was mind-blowingly erotic, if only she knew. Which she didn't. That he could tell by the panicked incredulity on her face.

'Under consideration?' Katy decided to ignore the second question totally. She also decided to stop craning her neck upwards to look at him because his gleaming, dark-as-night eyes were only dragging her down further and further. She concentrated on his chest instead, which was almost as bad.

He gave an elegant half-shrug. 'I have decided that there's no point rushing into marriage after all. And perhaps Isobel isn't quite the perfect life mate I had imagined.'

'But I thought…' Katy began, keen to explore this new development and even keener to get off the subject of her wayward body. 'I *thought* that she had all the *essential* qualities that made her the *ideal* wife?'

Bruno released her, giving her time to think, stupidly, that she now missed that sizzling electric current that seemed to flow straight from the palms of his hands through her wrists and into her body.

'Not quite *all*,' Bruno drawled with a veiled expression. He stuck his hands into his pockets, slid his eyes over her shoulder to where Joseph was still blissfully dozing, and then back to her bemused face.

'Oh, right.' Bewildered, Katy tried to imagine what exactly Isobel lacked and then proceeded to deduce that if Isobel *lacked* anything, then Bruno was looking for the impossible, because with love removed from the equation, then she certainly had all the necessary requirements on paper. She could only assume that Joseph's reaction had been telling enough for his godson to have second thoughts. Because there was no doubt that if Bruno had any love to distribute, then it was securely distributed onto one person, namely his godfather.

'Aren't you going to ask me what the missing link is?'

'Okay,' Katy obliged, 'what's the missing link?'

'This.'

In the space of a split second, she knew what he was going to do and it was as if the slow burn of excitement inside her had licked its steady flame against dry tinder, sending everything into a vortex of supercharged heat. Katy thought that she might even have given a slight

moan although she couldn't be sure because time seemed
to have stopped and, with it, her awareness of everything
around her. There were just the two of them in this intense zone and as his dark head descended her lips parted
without any deliberate thought on her part. Her body had
moved into a state of hungry compliance and every sense
in her was lost as she felt the warm touch of his mouth
against hers, covering it, then turning a gentle kiss into
something hard and demanding and unstoppable. He
moved one hand to cup the nape of her neck and the
other curved around her waist, pulling her into him until
there was no mistaking the hard throbbing of his arousal
pressed against her. With a whimper of complete and
utter surrender, Katy reached up and coiled her fingers
into his hair.

As his prying tongue delved into her mouth, Katy forgot everything. She forgot where she was; she forgot
Joseph resting in a chair only yards away from them; she
forgot that Bruno was a man no sane woman should get
involved with unless they had a deep-down suicide wish.

The door being pushed open only dimly penetrated her
consciousness and it was only when, eyes blissfully
closed, she felt Bruno pull away sharply from her that
she came to her senses and blankly looked where he was
now looking. Namely at Isobel whose face was a picture
of stony, thunderous fury.

Before she could open her mouth, Bruno was striding
towards her. At which point the reality, which Katy had
happily relegated to the back of her mind, reared up in
all its grim detail and she looked desperately around to
see that Joseph still had his eyes shut.

How he could continue dozing through what had happened was beyond her. True, they hadn't been shouting
or making any noise, but she wondered that some of the

electrifying thickness of the atmosphere hadn't wafted across to him and woken him up.

Uncertain, she remained where she was, watching as Bruno led Isobel out of the room in a vice-like grip, then very quickly she snatched up her robe and covered herself with it.

Leaving Joseph on his own was not an option. If he woke up to find her gone, he might panic, become disorientated. She imagined him stumbling into the pool in confusion and gently shook him.

'Time for us to head in, Joseph.' Did her voice sound normal? She hazarded a smile and then wondered whether it looked convincing. Her mind was whirling at what had just happened. Bruno had kissed her and she had felt as though she had suddenly been catapulted into orbit. There had been no question of resisting. She had just succumbed. One hundred per cent.

'Are you all right, my dear? You look a little...*fazed*.' He was finding it hard not to grin or at least toss her some little cliché about young people blithely assuming that the old were good for nothing except maybe dozing in a chair by a pool while they couldn't keep their hands off one another. It had been something of a surprise when he had blinked open his eyes and watched the scenario being played out in front of him and he had been on the verge of leaping up, if his bones would enable him to do anything as energetic as leaping, so that he could interrupt, but he hadn't. He might be an old man but he knew mutual attraction when he saw it. Thinking about it, he had seen glimpses of it ever since he had gone into hospital and they had come visiting and he knew better than to try and intervene with his pontificating. And besides, what was there to pontificate about? Bruno and Katy were his two favourite people in his life, and he could think of nothing better than seeing them together. Bruno was not suited to Isobel. He only imagined he was.

'Fazed?' Katy produced a jolly laugh from somewhere. 'What about?'

Joseph took refuge in a mumble and allowed himself to be helped back to the house, observing how he was guided as far as possible from the sitting room, where hopefully his godson was coming to his senses and dispatching the viper without delay.

'Where is Bruno and…and…oh, dear, I seem to have forgotten the lady's name…old age, you know…'

Katy looked at him with raised eyebrows. She was already feeling calmer with Joseph at her side. Something about his tranquillity was rubbing itself off on her.

'Her name's Isobel, Joseph, as you well know. And they're somewhere around…' She waved one hand vaguely to encompass the part of the house where they weren't.

'Perhaps we should go and see them. Only polite.'

'Oh, no,' Katy said hurriedly. 'They…they're probably *busy*. We'll see them a bit later.' She imagined Joseph bumbling into one great, big, swirling shouting match and shuddered. Isobel's face had not promised a calm reaction to what she had seen. Her lover and the home help, as Katy well knew she considered her, in a clinch. She would never, ever, have thought that she would have the starring role in a situation like that and she was horribly, *guiltily*, aware that it had been her fault. She had allowed Bruno to kiss her and she had flung herself into the kiss with fervent excitement, instead of shoving him away.

Her guilt grew with every step she took and, when she had finally established Joseph in the conservatory with a cup of tea and the newspaper, she was convinced that leaving Bruno to deal exclusively with Isobel's wrath was all wrong. It might take all the courage at her disposal, but she felt morally compelled to at least set Isobel straight on one score. That their embrace had meant nothing, that it had been something that had happened out of the blue and would never be repeated. What she chose to do with the information was her business.

'Where are you off to now?' Joseph demanded as she headed in the direction of the door. 'You're behaving like a cat on a hot tin roof!'

'Oh. To, you know, change. Have a bath. I'm still in my swimsuit.' Joseph had used the changing room by the pool and was already in his trousers and neat collared shirt, as fresh as a daisy. 'And I thought I might just, you know, see whether Bruno and Isobel wanted something to drink. Some tea, perhaps.'

'Tea? Most normal people are having something a little stronger at this time of the evening.'

'Well, something a little stronger then. Wine.'

He gave an elaborate sigh, nodded, and Katy scooted out of the room and across the hall, walking steadily in the direction of the sitting room and resisting the urge to turn tail and dash up the stairs. She should really have a bath and change before she confronted them but she knew that if she headed up to her bedroom, chances were high that she would chicken out of doing what she felt she had to do.

She heard their voices before she hit the door but at least they weren't shouting. Actually, she couldn't picture Bruno ever shouting but neither was Isobel. And there were no ominous sounds of things being hurled the width of the room. Maybe they had kissed and made up.

If that was the case, then problem solved, Katy told herself firmly. She wouldn't have to explain anything and she could return to being the hired help who had happened, for five minutes, to have a body that had sparked Bruno's curiosity. She took a very deep breath, then she knocked on the door and pushed it open at the same time.

Two pairs of eyes swivelled in her direction. Bruno looked incredibly calm. He was standing nonchalantly by the window with a drink in one hand. She had no idea what was going through his head because his expression was shuttered and unrevealing. On the other hand, she had every idea what was going through Isobel's head and it struck Katy that, despite the lack of shouting, the other woman was very, very angry. Her eyes were like chips of ice and her mouth was an indrawn line of suppressed rage.

'What the hell are *you* doing here?' Isobel spat out, taking two steps towards the door. Katy clung to the door handle until her knuckles were white.

'I wanted to explain…'

'There's no need,' Bruno drawled without moving or raising his voice. 'This has nothing to do with you.'

Katy felt as though he had slapped her on the face, but she stood her ground although some of her resolve, admittedly, was wavering. A little voice was having a laugh at her expense, asking how she could have imagined herself to be anything but a bit player in the unfolding drama. That kiss had meant nothing to Bruno. It certainly would not have affected his feelings or lack of them towards Isobel.

'*Nothing to do with her?*' Isobel's head whipped around and she narrowed her eyes at the casually lounging figure by the window. 'You invite me up here *to meet your godfather*, you lead me to think that we might actually be going somewhere with this relationship, and then I find you slobbering over the *staff*?'

Bruno looked icily at her. 'It's over, Isobel. Frankly, I can't see what else there is to say on the subject.'

It was such a witheringly blunt put-down that Katy felt a momentary pang of compassion for Isobel. She might not be Mother Teresa in disguise but she would still be suffering the humiliation of catching her man in the arms of another woman. She tentatively stepped into the room, towelling robe tightly wrapped around her, and cleared her throat.

'I just want to say, Isobel, that what you witnessed, well, meant nothing...'

'Do you really expect me to *believe that*?' She had turned completely away from Bruno and, frankly, Katy didn't blame her. His expression was cold and forbidding and very scary.

'It's the truth!'

'You've been closeted in this place for *weeks*, so-called *working*, and you expect me to believe that on the *one* day I happen to come up, you just find yourselves in each other's arms, snogging one another like two teenagers?' She ended this on a choked sob, which she obviously found infuriating because she raised one clenched fist and pressed it against her mouth.

'Well, yes!'

'I can't believe it.' Furious eyes fastened onto Bruno. 'I can't believe you could be *such a bastard*. I can't believe you could string me along *for months* and then waltz into the arms of someone else, *the home help, for God's sake*, without a backward glance.'

'Leave Katy out of this,' was all he said, in a very low voice.

'How can I? *You* obviously couldn't!' She grabbed her little bag from the chair and pulled herself up to her immense height. 'Well, don't think for a minute that *you're going to get away with this*! I'm not *just anybody*, Bruno Giannella. You might have got away with walking all over women in the past, but this time *you picked the wrong one*!'

Katy pressed herself against the wall and listened to this vicious speech with horror. Whatever Bruno said, *she* was responsible for this, with her girlish infatuation and lack of self-control. Okay, maybe he *had* come to the conclusion that he had made a mistake, but if they hadn't been caught *in flagrante*, the tenor of this breakup would have been completely different. Isobel wouldn't have been standing there making threats and meaning them, from the sounds of it.

'Really.' He sounded mildly interested. 'And what do you intend to do?'

Isobel was reduced to enraged silence.

'Hire a hit man to kill me and save the rest of the female population from my hideous exploits? Sneak into my apartment and chop the sleeves off all my shirts?' He lowered his fabulous eyes for the briefest of seconds. 'Report my dastardly behaviour to the press?'

Katy gasped and tried to imagine all of those possibilities. She snapped out of her reverie to hear Isobel swooshing towards her and watched as she strode towards the door with a tight smile on her face.

'We'll see,' she said in a voice that could curdle milk. 'But—' she paused to look at him, only inches away from Katy '—you'd be stupid to underestimate a scorned woman. As for you—' she glanced down at Katy '—good luck. He might be a stallion in bed but don't bank on anything more than a spot of good sex.'

Katy found that she was shaking as Isobel swept out of the room. With just the two of them now in the room, she was acutely conscious of her dress but she couldn't possibly dash upstairs to her bedroom with the risk of bumping into Isobel on the way out. She stared mutely at Bruno and then finally whispered, 'I'm really sorry.'

'Are you? Interesting. What for?'

'For…'

'Like I said, you didn't have anything to do with us breaking up so there's no need to beat yourself up with a guilty conscience.' He pushed himself away from the window and sat down on one of the chairs. 'Where's Joseph?'

'In the conservatory. You were very unkind to her, Bruno.'

Bruno looked at her in disbelief. 'Me? Unkind? What on earth are you talking about? And why don't you sit down? Before you fall down?'

Katy sat and worriedly leant forward. 'And what if she *does* try and do something…well…get even, so to speak…?'

'What are we talking about here? The threats or my unkindness?'

'Well, both, actually. I just think that you were so dismissive of her.' Katy frowned earnestly at him and chewed her lip. 'You just stood there and let her rant and rave without even trying to calm her down…it must have been awful for her to…well, you know…'

'If you'd come in a bit earlier, you would have heard my efforts to calm her down. Isobel wasn't open to being calmed down. Nor was she open to my explanation for the breakup. She didn't want to hear that it might have been her fault in any way. She wanted a scapegoat. The fact is I came to my senses and realised that what she and I had just wasn't quite good enough to last a lifetime, however good it all sounded in theory.'

'So you were wrong.'

'But big enough to admit it.' He gave her a slow, crooked smile that sent that terrible, treacherous shiver through her all over again.

'Right.' She stood up and avoided his eyes. 'I'd better go and change and start thinking about dinner. I guess Isobel's going back to London...'

'And I doubt she'll be popping in to say goodbye.'

'How can you be so *cool*?' Katy asked with genuine bewilderment. Her two serious relationships had been mutually ended, but she had still agonised over the details—but then she kept forgetting that Bruno wasn't like a normal human being.

'I did us both a favour.' He shrugged and looked away from her. 'What Isobel needs is a very-well connected, very subservient man with plenty of family money and an over-developed desire to please. In the long run, I would have driven her crazy. It worked for a while because, when I think about it, we never spent any long periods of time together and we certainly never did the mundane things that most normal couples do. I was never around for long enough because of work demands.'

He almost made it sound as though Isobel had been unreasonable to have reacted the way she did. 'And you don't feel a bit jittery about her threats?'

'She doesn't possess a key to the apartment,' Bruno said, stretching his long legs out in front of him, 'so she won't be able to sneak in and shred my suits and I doubt even Isobel would be vengeful enough to pay someone to bump me off.' He appeared to find the thought of that amusing.

'And what about reporting you to the press...?' Before she could stop feeling somehow to blame, Katy knew that she had to clear up these loose threads because she didn't want Bruno to be hurt because of her. Even though she knew that he was probably incapable of being hurt by anyone. Still…

'Well, I *am* a public figure, I guess…' He rested his head against the back of the chair and half closed his eyes. 'But a very private man. But you needn't worry. Isobel was speaking in the heat of the moment. By the time she gets to London, she'll have calmed down and by next week she'll be counting her blessings and announcing to the world that she's well rid of me…'

Joseph certainly didn't hide the fact that he considered his godson well rid of the bountiful blonde. With Katy, he was more open about his misgivings about any relationship they might have been nurturing, although over dinner, with Bruno, he was more circumspect in his musings, only saying that she hadn't seemed to be the right type for his godson. When pressed by Bruno for a definition of what he considered his *right type*, Joseph was uncharacteristically reticent.

Katy made very sure not to involve herself in this conversation. She couldn't begin to contribute anyway since she didn't know the first thing about men like Bruno. Not a mention had been made about that kiss they had shared by the pool. After Isobel had stormed out of the room, she had half expected him to say something about what had taken place between them, but not a word and his silence on the subject had been telling enough for her to steer well clear of it. She propped her chin in her hands and as male voices faded into vague background noise she allowed herself to go over in her head that wonderful sensation of when his mouth had met hers. Her head told her that she was pathetic even thinking about it, but her heart was all for an action replay. When she realised that Bruno and Joseph had lapsed into silence, she flushed and stood up to clear the dishes.

'Leave them,' Bruno commanded. 'Let's retire to the sitting room and have a drink. I think I need one.'

Katy eyed the nearly finished bottle of wine, which he had single-handedly demolished.

'A decent drink,' he amended, reading her mind.

'You two go ahead,' Katy said. 'Course, Joseph, you'll be sticking to fruit juice...'

'Possibly,' Joseph grumbled. 'Though I'm sure it's not very good for my digestive system. Too much fruit juice isn't, you know.'

Katy impulsively walked towards him and fondly kissed the top of his head. 'I never knew you had a degree in medicine.'

Joseph grasped her hand and gave it a little squeeze. 'Adorable, isn't she?' he said smugly. 'I'll stick to the fruit juice provided you don't scuttle upstairs without saying goodnight!'

Katy was just happy to scuttle off to the kitchen and away from Bruno, and managed to take an extraordinarily long time tidying the table and washing up the dishes and then putting everything away even though she could just as easily have loaded the dishwasher.

By the time she was ready to head for the sitting room, she had convinced herself of two very important things. The first was that Bruno was not physically attracted to her, merely curious, and the second was that all she felt for him was good old-fashioned lust and the reason she had been so flustered in the first place was because lust had never been something she had experienced in her life before. It had leapt out at her from nowhere. There was no reason to feel all hot and bothered because her body was behaving in an odd way. Lust was something she could control!

There was a new spring in her step when she finally

made it to the sitting room almost two hours later only to find that Bruno was there on his own and of Joseph there was no sign.

'He was tired. I took him to bed.' He hadn't bothered to switch on the overhead light and as a consequence the room was bathed in shadows thrown off by the two table lamps.

'You should have called me.'

'I think I'm capable of getting my own godfather sorted out, Katy. Besides, you were being a martyr by spring-cleaning the house.'

'I was not being a martyr!' He had said he wanted a drink and he had had a few from the looks of it. He sounded completely sober, but there was a half-empty bottle of whisky on the small circular table next to him and his long body was stretched out on the sofa in an attitude of total relaxation.

He was missing Isobel, she decided, more than he would ever admit, had had too much to drink and was now in a mood to start taking digs at her. He looked as though he had been ceaselessly raking his fingers through his hair and the tousled look lent him a boyish, vulnerable air. She wanted to smooth it down and say something that would wipe that brooding expression off his face.

She also wanted to escape from the suffocating turmoil that was springing up inside her. Consequently, she neither moved forward nor did she walk out. She remained where she was in a state of suspended agitation while he continued to look at her through half-closed lids.

'Okay, then,' he agreed, 'not a martyr. Maybe just avoiding me. Mmm. Yes. Avoiding me. I think I'd go for that explanation.' He fumbled on the table for his glass and drained what was left in it while staring at her over the rim. 'But why would you be avoiding me? An enigma, wouldn't you agree? Unless, of course...' he let the words drip slowly from his lips, then he flashed her a wicked, heart-stopping smile '...it's because I touched you...is that the reason, Katy?'

Katy wanted to swoon. Now she knew exactly how those Victorian maidens felt. Rapidly beating heart, wobbly legs, faint perspiration.

'Come here and sit by me and we'll talk about it.'

'I haven't given it a second's thought,' she lied, 'and you ought to stop drinking.'

'I won't touch another mouthful if you come and sit here by me.' He raised his arms and folded them behind his head and proceeded to watch her.

Katy took a few tentative steps towards him. The closer she got, the stronger was the pull she felt to keep going, until she was standing just in front of him.

Bruno shifted slightly to the right, to make room for her, and then patted the vacated spot on the sofa.

'Sit down. Here. Nice warm spot.'

Katy perched.

'I'm really sorry about Isobel,' she began, her soft heart melting at what she felt must be some hidden pain that had driven him to the bottle.

'Why? You didn't like her.'

'I wouldn't say that *I didn't like her*. She was just very, very different from me. A little scary, actually. Especially being so *tall*.' Katy had felt like a pygmy next to her.

'Okay. She was scary then. So why do you feel sorry about her? Forgot that she tried to threaten me? Anyway, as I've told you, I had a narrow escape. You should be feeling relieved at the thought of that.'

'Well, yes, I suppose...' Katy looked at him, marvelling abstractedly at the length of his eyelashes, of all things. 'Although, it's always sad when a relationship ends, isn't it? Course, you probably don't feel the same way about that as most normal people,' she confided thoughtfully, 'since you must have been through thousands of relationships that ended.'

'Thanks a lot for that,' Bruno said moodily. 'One of the things I find most enchanting with you is your ability to tell the truth, the whole truth and nothing but the truth. A man who has had thousands of passing relationships can certainly count himself as very successful, can't he, at the pinnacle of the totem pole?'

'Sorry.'

'Yes? Are you?' Brooding black eyes scanned her face with deliberate, slow consideration and Katy nodded helplessly. He wasn't slurring his words but he had thrown her with his burst of honesty. She nodded again, this time with a bit more conviction and watched him smile lazily back at her. 'How sorry?'

'Sorry about what happened and sorry about speaking, well, out of turn...' There was something oddly exciting about the way he was staring at her. Maybe that glitter in his eyes was the drink. Katy hadn't had much experience when it came to communicating with people under the influence of alcohol. Her parents cracked open the occasional bottle of wine when guests were over, and there was always sherry at Christmas, but she had led a quiet, sheltered life that did not include whisky-drinking.

'Forgiven.' He laughed softly under his breath and then reached out one hand so that he could stroke her wrist.

Katy felt the delicate touch of his finger with a rush of powerful sexual awareness and guiltily realised that she had been waiting for him to touch her. No, *longing* for it. That lust thing again. She parted her lips on a soft,

helpless sigh and her body relaxed, as if invisible strings
that had been holding it up had gone slack.

'I should go,' she heard herself stammer and then he
was sitting up towards her. The sofa depressed and she
felt herself sliding towards him, a collision of body
against body.

'Go?' Bruno nuzzled softly into her ear. 'That's not
what I have in mind... Oh, no, what I have in mind is
taking up where we left off...'

CHAPTER SEVEN

'TAKING up where we left off?' Katy's heart was racing as she contemplated the possibilities of what Bruno was saying to her.

'No good you slipping back into these voluminous dresses,' he chided mockingly. 'Too late to try and hide that body of yours.' As if to emphasise the point he was making, his hand curved into her waist, then along her back, travelling upwards until it found the nape of her neck, then he pulled her towards him.

Katy half fell onto him and felt the hardness of his torso. He had been right about the voluminous dress. She had worn it as protection, something to deter any glances that might be inclined to linger.

'I wasn't…Bruno, no…hang on…'

'Stop talking. Kiss me. "Kiss me, Kate".' He grinned at his witticism and she felt the corners of her mouth tug into a smile.

Watching her, Bruno marvelled at how he had managed to miss the soft perfection of her lips all these months that he had been visiting his godfather and seeing her in passing. Her mouth was soft and full and delicately pink. He drew her closer and stifled a groan of pleasure as he prised them open, very gently, and felt her melt beneath him. Her tongue was hesitant, at first, but not for long. She returned his kiss with sweet surrender and her slight body curved into his. A perfect fit.

She only pulled back to say, with a frown, 'I'm taking advantage of you.'

That almost made him laugh out loud but he remained perfectly grave. 'I'm a big boy, Katy. I think it's fair to say that I wouldn't let you take advantage of me if I didn't want it. Desperately.'

Desperately? Katy wondered if she had misheard him.

'You've had too much to drink…you're not in control…'

'I'm in perfect control. In fact,' he added expansively, 'I don't think I've ever been in as much control in my life before.' He traced the contours of her mouth with his tongue and felt her shiver against him. 'I haven't been drinking here on my own all night,' Bruno confessed. 'One glass of whisky. The bottle was pretty much finished by the time I got to it.' He kissed her jawline, then tilted her head back so that he could do the same to the slender column of her neck. 'I haven't been drowning lots of hidden pain in drink,' he murmured. 'Do you still feel sorry for me?'

'No, I don't!' Katy responded sternly.

'Good. I'd hate the thought of a woman making love with me because she felt sorry for me…'

His words sent a flood of hot, pulsing excitement racing through her.

'Make love…?'

'But not here.' He traced her cheekbones with his fingers, then trailed them along her collar-bone, dipping under the break of her dress, which was so modestly high that they were barred entry to her soft cleavage. On one level, he certainly hadn't been lying when he'd told her he was in control. Right now he was only just managing to hang onto that control by the skin of his teeth.

'Not here?' Katy whispered faintly.

'Comfortable as this sofa is, I still prefer the thought

of making love in my king-sized bed. Call me old fash-
ioned.'

'Oh, goodness!'

'Is that an appropriate reaction, I wonder?' He added
quirky to her growing list of character traits.

'But Joseph's upstairs!'

'And, fortunately, tucked up in his own bedroom. Shall
I carry you up the stairs?'

'Don't be silly!' Katy stood up and watched as Bruno
followed suit. He looked a little dishevelled, with his shirt
untucked from the waistband of his trousers and his feet
bare. He had obviously kicked off his loafers somewhere
along the line. Dishevelled but still incredibly beautiful.

Going up the stairs, he held her hand. The house was
silent. There was no sound coming from Joseph's room
and there was no light peeping out from under the door.
They walked quietly along the darkened corridor and entered the bedroom with which Katy was quite familiar.
She had cleaned it once after he had gone, when Maggie
had been off work, and she frequently popped in to make
sure the dust wasn't gathering and it was aired.

The big difference was that at no point had she ever
been in it at the same time as he had.

Even vacant, his bedroom had still had the power to
destabilise her. She had not once gone into it without her
head filling up with images of him. Here, now, with him
standing right by her side and softly shutting the door
behind them, Katy almost yelped with the enormity of
what she was doing. Her face felt as hot as fire and her
hands were trembling. She stuck them behind her back
and clasped them tightly together.

The overhead light in the bedroom was operated on a
dimmer switch. Bruno had turned it down to the lowest
so that the room was bathed in a mellow glow.

He began unbuttoning his shirt, watching her, and Katy stared in fascination. Warmth pooled inside her, making her breathing sluggish.

'Look,' she began in a voice she barely recognised, 'there's something I have to tell you...' Why had she ever underestimated the power of animal attraction? Being in Bruno's company had finally taken its toll. Under the continual impact of his sexual aura, her own natural defences had crumbled. Why else would she be standing here, with her feet rooted to the ground like blocks of lead and her disobedient body urging her to things that her mind, when it was working, would have recoiled at in horror?

Bruno's body stilled. 'What's that?'

Katy looked at him in mute silence for a few seconds. 'I expect you think that...well...I know that the kinds of circles you move in...'

'Oh, no, you're not about to embark on one of those never-ending, circular explanations of yours, are you?'

'What do you mean?'

'I mean,' Bruno said, trying to restrain himself, 'that you need to stop beating about the bush and get to the point of what you're going to say.' A surge of massive frustration swept over him like a tidal wave of freezing cold water. He knew what was coming. Confronted with the reality of what was looming up in front of them, naked body against naked body, she was going to make her excuses and leave. He wondered what he would do and realised, with disgust, that he had to yank himself back from the temptation to beg. He had never begged for any woman in his life and he had never felt the inclination to. He wasn't about to start now either. His lips narrowed into a grim line and he folded his arms across his impressive, muscular chest.

'What I'm *saying*...' At this point, Katy just wanted the floor to open up and swallow her and her embarrassment up. She licked her lips nervously and tried to focus on his face even though his magnificent body was like a magnet to her eyes. 'What I'm *saying* is that I'm not like those other women...'

'What other women?' He took a couple of steps towards her and Katy held her ground.

'The other women you've slept with in the past!' she burst out in one breath. 'Women like Isobel! Sophisticated, experienced women! I'm not like them, Bruno. I know you're going to find this ridiculous but I'm a virgin!'

Bruno looked at her and nothing came out. Katy, her defences reassembling themselves with gathering speed, couldn't help but think that this was the first time and probably the last time that she would ever see Bruno Giannella literally struck dumb.

Well, who could blame him? What woman of her age had never slept with a man before? Hadn't even been tempted to, come to it, until now. She had never felt this weird, wonderful, burning desire for anyone that she felt for this big man standing in front of her in stunned silence.

'Crazy, isn't it?' she said, just to break the unbearable silence. Of course, she knew why he hadn't said anything. Because Bruno, man of the world that he was, master of whatever woman he wanted, *a stallion in bed*, no less, according to his ex-girlfriend, would not be overjoyed at the prospect of taking a virgin to bed. He probably wanted someone who *knew* how to make love.

'I'm not sure,' Bruno said in a very unsteady voice, 'that *crazy* is the word I would use to describe it.' He took a couple more steps towards her so that he was now standing inches away. Katy inhaled deeply and breathed in his unique, sexy, masculine scent.

'What would you say, then?' she muttered in self-derision. 'Sad? Pathetic? Unbelievable? You don't have to pretend that it doesn't change things, Bruno. I know it does.'

'Explain.'

'Well, a man like you…'

She looked down and he tilted her chin up very gently so that he could meet her eyes. He really didn't suppose that he should tell her what her revelation had done to him. That right now he felt like a man who'd suddenly discovered the winning lottery ticket stuck at the back of a drawer. That he wanted to crow with sheer masculine glee.

'You suppose too much,' he said softly instead. 'You needn't be afraid. I intend to be very, very gentle with you…'

'Could we turn the lights off?'

'Absolutely not.' Her dress was a maidenly affair, with small pearl buttons all the way down the front and, typically, each button was done up, right up to the little cream collar that had deterred his wandering fingers earlier on in the evening. He started with the top button and his eyes didn't leave her face as he proceeded his way down until he had reached the waist.

Then he kissed her until he felt her nerves dissipating. Her hands reached up to curl around his neck. If she needed any proof that he was turned on then all she had to do was feel him through his trousers. He pulled her close and heard her little gasp as his arousal pressed against her, hard and throbbing and urgent.

He slid the dress free of her, where it pooled around her feet, and then held her hands in his, drawing them down to her sides and feasting his hungry eyes on her body. The same body that had been driving him crazy since she had revealed herself in that severe swimsuit. It hit him that in fact he had been looking at her even before then, had been watching her movements as she'd pottered around that office where they had been working, blithely unaware of his slumberous gaze on her.

Her underwear was simple, erotically simple. Plain white cotton bra, plain white cotton briefs that dipped beneath her belly button. Bruno reached up and tugged down the straps of the bra, then slid his hands behind her back to unclasp it. He half expected her to look down but she didn't.

The desire to cringe as her body was exposed never came. Instead, Katy felt wickedly provocative as her small breasts were finally released from their constraints, jutting out, the large nipples tightly peaked in anticipation. His eyes raked over her and, as if he couldn't stop himself, he reached out and touched one nipple with a look of wonder on his face.

'You have,' he said in a slightly shaky voice, 'fabulous breasts. Fabulous nipples.' He rubbed one with his thumb, then raised his other hand so that he was caressing them both, feeling their weight in his hands, teasing the buds with his thumbs.

Katy closed her eyes and tilted her head back, enjoying the fierce pleasure of having him touch her. When his mouth circled one of her sensitised nipples, she moaned and squirmed and sighed as he lifted her off her feet and deposited her on the bed.

Watching him remove the rest of his clothes made her ache even more between her legs and she had to fight the awful urge to touch herself. Her breathing quickened as he shrugged off his trousers and boxer shorts and revealed his impressive erection.

Then he moved onto the bed with her, his body over hers as he worked his way from her lips down.

He told her that there wasn't an inch of her that he didn't want to touch, although his words only half penetrated the haze of her own heated yearning. They were a low, husky rumble that sent her pulses leaping. He made her feel languorous and sexy and unashamed of her body and Katy, drinking at this fountain of desire for the first time in her life, lapped it up.

She caressed his head as he claimed her breasts, teasing them, sucking them, then moving lower so that he could trail wet kisses across her flat stomach. When he pulled down her briefs, she waited for him to enter her, knowing that she was no longer scared, but he didn't. Instead, shockingly, he began to explore the very core of her with his tongue, sliding it along her moist crease and then pushing apart her thighs so that he could feast on her honeyed moistness.

Katy's body jerked in immediate response and she arched back, writhing against his searching mouth.

When she half opened her eyes and saw the top of his dark head moving against her down there, his hands placed flatly on each of her inner thighs, she was so overcome by craving that she felt she might just pass out. She could feel her excitement building as he continued to lick her most intimate place.

Just when she thought that she wouldn't be able to hold out any longer against the need to reach her own fulfilment, Bruno moved away briefly so that he could take protective measures. It was the merest passage of seconds, then he covered her body with his, guiding himself into her but very slowly and very gently.

'Shh,' he murmured, as if she had said something, then he covered her mouth with his and began to build a steady rhythm to his thrusts.

Katy's body opened up like a flower to receive him and she began to move against him, picking up his rhythm until they were moving as one.

His body shuddered as he came into her and she responded with her own soaring climax that had her whirling away, flying out of space and out of time. When she finally landed and she opened her eyes, it was to find Bruno looking down at her with such tenderness that her heart constricted.

'Was it okay for you?' Katy ventured, with her usual honesty, and Bruno grinned and brushed some hair back from her face.

'The earth moved.' Literally. He couldn't explain it but she had managed to transport him in a way that had never happened before.

'Are you being sarcastic?'

He rolled off her and then stuck his arm under her head, pulling her close against him so that she was nestled into his neck.

It felt so comfortable that Katy promptly curved to her side and stretched her arm across his chest.

'I could fall asleep,' she confessed. In truth, she felt as if she were drifting along on ripples of contentment and peace.

'Try and restrain yourself,' Bruno said drily.

'I know. I have to get back to my own room. If Joseph knew what had taken place here, he'd die a thousand deaths.'

'What *has* happened here, Katy?' Bruno asked in husky undertone.

'You know as well as I do. We made love.' She was

bewildered that he would ask her a question with such
an obvious answer, then her brain clicked into gear and
she realised that what he was really talking about was
what their love-making had meant. Good Lord, was he
scared? Scared that she had given her virginity to him
and might now be nurturing thoughts of relationships and
commitment?

'I mean,' she expanded hastily, pulling back her arm
only to find him replacing it, 'we just gave in to…well,
that lust thing…'

'That lust thing.'

'Right,' Katy said eagerly. 'When you touch me, I just
melt. I can't seem to help myself. You don't have to
worry that I'm going to do anything stupid, Bruno, like
start having ideas about relationships or any such thing,
because I won't.'

He didn't say anything for such a long time that she
eventually propped herself up on one elbow and looked
down at him. 'I think I ought to get back to my bedroom
now.'

'We need to talk this one through a little more.'

'Why?' Did he think that he had to issue a few explicit
warnings about not getting involved with him?

'Why me?'

'Sorry?'

'Why me?' He crossed his arms behind his head and
proceeded to subject her to one of those cross-
examination stares that always made her feel hot and
bothered. 'How is it that you never got around to sleeping
with a man before?'

Katy could see where this was leading and it was exactly as she had feared. He would be thinking that he was
special to her and he was trying to prise that confession
out so that he could set the situation straight. She wished

that she could get angry with the implication and storm out of the room, thereby terminating her discomfiture, but, like a fool, she felt so unbearably good lying next to him that she just didn't want to leave. Well, not until she had ironed things out, she told herself.

'I don't know,' she said truthfully. 'I've really only had two serious relationships and neither of them got that far.'

Bruno gave a harsh, derisive laugh under his breath. 'Well, those must have been sizzling relationships if you never got around to *that lust thing.*'

Katy reckoned she could detect sarcasm as good as the next person and she promptly sat up, faced him and glared.

'They were very *nice* relationships!' she retorted defensively.

'So *nice* that you never managed to make it to the bed.' He shot her a smug smile and in return got a frosty look. 'It's very hard to concentrate on being serious when your breasts are on display,' Bruno informed her, and when she automatically raised her arms to shield them he pulled them down. 'No, no. Too late for modesty, my darling.' He touched the tip of one nipple with his finger and watched it tighten in immediate response.

'Not fair,' Katy protested.

'Tell me what went wrong with those losers.'

'They weren't *losers*. Neil was a student and it just fizzled out because we ended up only seeing each other when he was back from university.'

'You should have been panting to be in each other's arms.'

'We talked.'

Talked and talked and talked, Katy remembered. All about his new, exciting life at university, about the discos he went to, the thrilling people he mixed with. She had stopped being his girlfriend and had mutated into his confidante, sadly still stuck in their home town and lacking in the fun, fun, fun quality that every single university student appeared to possess. Katy hadn't minded and what had *that* said about things?

'Anyway, it just kind of faded away, then I met Paul...'

'And you did lots of talking...' For some reason this was music to his ears. He bounced one breast in his hand and then propped himself up so that he could suckle on a nipple that was just begging for a little attention.

'Are you listening?'

Bruno glanced up at her. 'Don't mind me.' Then he returned to the highly satisfying pleasure of sucking her other nipple. What was it about this woman that turned him on like an adolescent? Her body was as smooth as satin and perfectly formed. He felt himself hardening in anticipation of touching every inch of her all over again.

'I met Paul when I came to London... Bruno, I can't concentrate...'

'Good. You don't have to concentrate, my darling, on anyone aside from me.'

This time their love-making was slow and sensuous and Katy wanted it never to end. He guided her to him and then onto him, enjoying the delight she took in taking control. Her waist was so small that he could virtually span it with both his hands and aligned to her slightness was a suppleness and agility that he couldn't get enough of. She moved as gracefully as a dancer. Finally, spent, she lay on top of him and he stroked her hair, her neck, her back.

'I really must get back to my room,' Katy murmured

sleepily. 'You should have warned me that making love consumed so much energy.'

'You ain't seen nothing yet, my darling,' Bruno promised. 'And you can't go yet. You were in the process of telling me about loser number two before you distracted me.'

'Before *I* distracted *you*?' She rolled over to his side and made a determined effort not to wish for the impossible, not to long to be able to stay where she was, to fall asleep next to him and wake up alongside him in the morning, and…and…

With dismay, Katy found that her imagination was gathering momentum and that the things she longed to share with this man were going far beyond the one-night stand he needed and entering into the dangerous relationship territory that she had firmly denied wanting.

'Paul wasn't content with the hours I could give him.' She shrugged, winding up the explanation. 'I was an au pair at the time and I only had a certain amount of hours off during the week. Look, I'm not saying that this was a mistake or anything…'

'You seem to have headed off on another tangent.'

'But I want you to know that this…what we did…' She slipped her legs off the bed in one neat, unstoppable movement and stood up. If she had to gather her senses, then putting distance between them was step number one. Getting dressed would help as well. She didn't look at him as she began flinging on her clothes, although she knew that he was looking at her.

'We both gave in…'

'To the lust thing. I know. You've said that already. And look at me when I'm talking to you!'

Katy looked at him. She could do that now that she was safely ensconced in her clothes.

'I'm not going to hop into bed with you again, Bruno. Believe it or not, I'm not the kind of girl who does that...'

'So I gathered.'

'I know you think that because I'm attracted to you, I'm probably easy game...'

'Don't ever insinuate that I chase women just for the fun of it, Katy.' Hadn't he, though? In the past? Never getting involved, just enjoying the temporary pleasure and then moving on?

'Of course you do,' she answered and she could tell from his sudden dark flush that she had struck home. 'And there's no point trying to deny it. Bruno, your little escapades always made it to the gossip columns in the newspapers! You don't want commitment. You want never-ending fun and that's fine, but it's not for me.' His eyes were narrowing ominously as her speech progressed, but Katy knew that she had to speak her mind because if she left it all unsaid he would assume that he could pursue her while it suited him. She was attracted to him and, face it, she thought with brutal honesty, she was convenient. Here they were, both sharing the same house and, without Isobel on the scene to release his sexual energy, what easier than to turn to the little naïve country girl who had declared her weakness for him?

'And what *is* for you?' Bruno could feel her pulling away from him at a rate of knots and he didn't like it. He swept out of the bed, pausing on the way to snatch up his boxer shorts, which he stuck on, and then made sure to stand with his back to the door so that he was effectively barring her exit.

'You're in front of the door and I want to leave,' Katy protested with alarm.

'It's ridiculous to start running scared now,' he said by

way of response. 'We've made love and why kid ourselves that it's never going to happen again? We want
one another and I don't see anything wrong in that.
What's wrong in that?'

'You're trying to tie me up in knots.'

'I'm trying to get you to see sense.' Bruno wanted to
shake her. Anything to make her see what was as plain
as the nose on her face. They were consenting adults
whose bodies made music together. He could discern that
mulish stubbornness creeping over her and he knew with
gut-wrenching certainty that she was digging her heels
in.

'You're trying to get me to see *your* sense!'

'This argument would be all right if we hadn't just
spent the past three hours in each other's arms!'

'I don't want to be your plaything while you're up
here, Bruno. A little distraction on the side just for as
long as you're stuck here. Something to be tossed aside
when it's time to return to London and you spot bigger,
brighter, shinier toys waiting to be played with!'

'Whoever mentioned anything about tossing anyone
aside?'

'You don't have to!' Katy cried with heartfelt emotion.
'Your history speaks for itself!' She sighed and looked
down at her feet and willed herself not to cry. It took a
lot of effort, but eventually she looked up and said in a
calm, controlled voice, 'You can't stand there blocking
that door for ever. It's time for me to get back to my
room and there's nothing more to be said.'

'You're living in the wrong era,' Bruno said brusquely.
'Love, marriage…waiting for Mr Right to come along…
doesn't happen, Katy.'

She shrugged and he wanted to bellow at her that he

hated it when she ducked out of confrontation with one of those evasive shrugs of hers.

'I don't mind what lifestyle you choose, Bruno. You can work your way through the entire female population for all I care, but I'm not going to start giving myself away just for the fun of it!' Had she just told him that she didn't care? If he was even a little bit tuned in to women then he would see that for the nonsense that it was. She cared. Oh, how she cared.

Bruno slowly stepped aside, leant against the wall and folded his arms, like a dark Lucifer waiting to lure her back under his spell.

When Katy was right next to him, he said under his breath, 'We live and die by the choices that we make, Katy. Remember that. You may feel very virtuous and saint-like denying yourself a taste of fun in your zeal to find the right man to slip a ring on your finger, but be careful you don't end up wasting your life in one long, futile search.'

Katy's head filled with images of herself getting older, looking for Mr Might-be-just-round-the-corner and wishing that she'd been wise enough to take the offer Bruno had extended. He had a golden tongue and he had managed to paint her destiny in a frightening light. She swallowed down the temptation to give into the promise of sexual fulfilment that he had offered to her.

'Will you want me to work for you tomorrow?' she whispered miserably instead.

Bruno scowled and restlessly raked his fingers through his hair.

'Maybe in the afternoon,' he muttered grimly. 'I'll be out in the morning.'

Out? Katy thought. *Out where?*

'If you let me know what time—'

'I don't *know* what time!' Bruno exploded. He strode over to the easy chair by the window and deposited himself in it although his posture was far from comfortable. Every fibre of his body was giving off signals of frustrated, impotent rage. Katy found it hard to believe that those narrowed black eyes had softened with teasing tenderness on her only a short while earlier.

Where had it gone? she thought wretchedly. She left the room with a miserable feeling of having won the battle but lost the war. And it was made worse the following day because Bruno was nowhere to be seen.

'Business in London,' Joseph told her, when, at four in the afternoon, she casually mentioned his absence. 'Why?'

'Oh, no reason!' They were enjoying a walk in the garden. The weather was beautiful with the smell of early summer sifting through the trees and mingling with the smell of freshly mowed grass. Katy tried to enjoy the perfume and found instead that she was glaring down at the beds of flowers and thinking tortured thoughts of what precisely Bruno was doing in London.

'He was supposed to come back up at lunch time, but he phoned me earlier to say that he'd been delayed. Meetings, I expect.'

'I expect so. He's been here quite a while. He's probably getting back into the swing of things in London.' Fixing up hot dates with hot babes, she thought sourly, now that this damp squib had given him a resounding red light.

'Probably,' Joseph agreed. 'Guess you'll miss him being around when he finally does leave?'

'Oh, no! You and I can get back to normal, then. Carry on with the memoirs. We haven't visited the library in ages. Maybe we can go at the end of the week.' She was dreading getting back to the normality she had previously relished. Bruno had swept into her life like a tornado and shattered her peace and she didn't think she could ever get it back again.

If it had just been a question of lust, then, yes, this painful ache inside her would gradually ease and life would go back to what it had been before. Or something very similar anyway. But it wasn't just about lust, not for her. It was all about love and need and every other ludicrous word that she could never dare breathe to him. She had made the fatal error of falling in love with him and it served her right. Instead of recognising what she felt from early on and taking the necessary precautions, just as he had taken the necessary precautions when they had made love, she had hurled herself off the cliff with a great shout of joy and now she was left staring at a blank abyss for her sins.

'And we'll have to pick up the memoirs,' she said brightly to Joseph as they strolled towards the greenhouse. 'My typing skills are pretty good now. We can cover lots more! Well, I can type up what we cover a lot faster anyway!' She listened to herself babbling away frantically as they inspected the tomatoes and the grape vines and finally the orchids. By the time they made it back to the house she had covered every topic under the sun and Joseph had managed to slip in only the occasional word edgeways.

She found herself going back to the original topic they had briefly discussed earlier and, partly for Joseph's benefit but mostly for her own, she gravely reminded him that Bruno's extended day in London was the prelude to him leaving for good.

'He's probably missed the cut and thrust of big city life,' she expanded, imagining him cutting and thrusting with a series of dashing six-foot Isobel clones. 'This country life probably stifles him. No feverish excitement in the office, no phones ringing all the time, no important people calling in for…for financial advice or whatever…' No clubs, she amended in her head, no sizzling night life, no expensive restaurants full of famous, beautiful people who would naturally be on first name terms with him…

'He seems to rather like it up here,' Joseph said mildly, to which Katy heard herself give an uncharacteristically crazed laugh. 'The countryside has charms of its own,' he continued. 'There's no exchange for tranquillity and the inner peace that comes from being surrounded by Nature.'

Which was why she was so deeply fond of Joseph, Katy thought to herself. How could she possibly disillusion him with her own version of the truth? Which was that there was no conceivable reason for his godson to remain here when his purpose was fast coming to an end. Joseph was getting stronger by the day. Tranquillity and inner peace were words Bruno would never consider in his vocabulary.

She endured the remainder of the day, little knowing how life could change in a matter of a few short hours…

CHAPTER EIGHT

JOSEPH'S friend Dave Harrington was picking Joseph up at eight-thirty in the morning. He had a full morning planned, which included taking Joseph to the hospital for a routine check-up, followed by a few rounds of bridge at the rather swanky club on the outskirts of the town that offered tremendously good rates for old-age pensioners. Or, as Joseph called them, duffers with a bit of money and a lot of spare time who could be shoved into a couple of rooms that wouldn't have been in use otherwise during the day. Then a spot of lunch, with all the old cronies there.

'You can sleep in, my dear,' were Joseph's last words before he retired for bed the evening before. 'You deserve it, all the hard work you've been putting in with Bruno as taskmaster.'

Katy had protested dutifully but had been happy enough to give in without too much persuasion. She felt exhausted and it had nothing to do with hard work. All the activity taking place in her brain was tiring her. She was in love with Bruno and she had no idea what to do about it. Should she leave? Quit her job? If she stayed, she would inevitably continue to bump into him whenever he came to visit his godfather. She would never have the time and space for her feelings to wither away. One accidental meeting with him and everything, every longing, would flare right back into vigorous life and she would be left nursing scars only for them to re-open the minute he returned the next time.

But then, when she thought about leaving, she imagined a wretched existence, a lifetime of missing him and wanting him, and then that option didn't seem too good either.

Or perhaps she should simply cave in and have an affair with him, enjoy what he was offering and put off the inevitable heartache for as long as possible. But wouldn't that be worse? He would tire of her, ditch her and then, on top of everything else, she would have to contend with feeling like a failure.

It had been after midnight before she had finally fallen into a restless sort of sleep, punctuated with vivid, unsatisfactory dreams.

It took her a few minutes to realise that the knocking on her bedroom door was not a continuation of yet another unsettling dream with no particular ending.

It was Joseph and he looked far too bright-eyed for her liking, although that too took a few seconds to appreciate as she stared at him bleary-eyed, hair hanging in a tousled mane around her face.

'What time is it?' Katy asked, blinking.

'Eight!'

'Is there a problem with Dave?' Her brain began functioning a little more efficiently and she noticed that Joseph was fully dressed. 'Do you need me to give you a ride in? I'll just get changed. Sorry. I'm normally up so early. Give me a few minutes.'

'You little devil!'

'Wha..?'

'Course I *knew* it. Sensed it. Might be old but I'm not yet a fool!' He was beaming in a manner that sent a few shivers of alarm running down her spine.

What on earth was he talking about?

'Mind if I come in, Katy? Won't be long. Dave'll be

here any minute if he doesn't oversleep. You know these old people.' He chuckled and edged his way into her room so that he could plop himself comfortably in her reading chair by the fireplace. 'All that chat about Bruno leaving, getting me prepared. You should have come clean with me! No...I guess you were worried about how I would receive the news, but, my dear, there was no need! I can't tell you how delighted I am! Now, I *thought* you were looking a little flushed yesterday. *Not your usual self.* Very observant I can be, at times, you have to admit it!'

Katy had not the faintest idea what he was talking about. She slipped on her dressing gown, and perched herself on the edge of her bed.

'You're delighted,' she said, testing the water. 'I'm delighted that you're delighted.' *But what at?* she wondered, thinking fast and coming up blank.

'Of course, I shall miss you terribly. Hmm. Might have to leave this old place...can't imagine getting a replacement for you, my dear. Wouldn't be the same.'

'Replacement?' Now she was beginning to feel as if she had been tossed onto a roller coaster, destination unknown. 'I wasn't thinking of leaving, Joseph.' Well, she had been, true, but how on earth could Joseph have read her mind to that extent? Had she unwittingly said something yesterday? Out loud? She frowned, thinking back, wondering if she had let anything slip about what she was feeling.

'Naturally, *not yet.*' He beamed and looked · at his watch. 'Lord, look at the time! I'm going to have to go, my dear, but I just wanted you to know that you've made an old man very happy indeed!'

'By planning to leave?' Katy asked, deeply hurt.

Joseph, on his feet, took both her hands in his and gave

them a comforting squeeze. 'You're emotional, I know. It's an emotional time. But it's *right*. I have a gut feeling! You and Bruno are perfectly suited! And I'm so deeply overjoyed that you've decided to get married!'

He almost bounced out of the room, leaving Katy staring at the door in dumbfounded shock.

Marrying Bruno? Where on earth could he have got that idea from? Was this some weird complication following his heart attack? Hallucinations?

She was fully awake now and dressed quickly, barely stopping to give her hair a brush. Ten minutes later, she was pelting down the stairs, straight into the kitchen where Bruno was sitting at the kitchen table with an assortment of newspapers in front of him, a cup of coffee and a glass of juice.

Katy skidded to a halt and every confused thought drained out of her as she absorbed him sitting there. He had pushed himself away from the table so that he could extend his long legs out in front of him. The sleeves of his shirt were rolled up to the elbows and he had his fingers loosely linked together on his lap. He was so ferociously sexy that she heard her own audible gasp.

'Coffee?' He pointed to the glass filter jug behind her on the kitchen counter. 'I've just made some.'

'When did you get back?' She wondered whether Bruno had been privy to any of his godfather's surreal ramblings. If he hadn't, then she would just have to wait by the front door until Joseph returned, kidnap him and tell him, very gently of course, that he had got the wrong end of the stick from somewhere.

She felt a little calmer because Bruno certainly didn't seem to be flustered, which he would have been had he listened in to what Joseph had told her ten minutes earlier.

'Very early this morning, as a matter of fact.'

'And I guess you haven't…seen your godfather? Before he left, I mean. He's gone out with Dave Harrington.' She turned her back and made a performance of pouring herself a mug of coffee, while she held her breath and waited for his reply.

'Oh, yes, I saw him all right.'

The silence stretched on and on until Katy finally turned around to find Bruno looking at her. 'I think you ought to have a look at these newspapers,' he said conversationally, and, without taking his eyes away from her face, he swivelled one of the tabloids so that it was pointing in her direction.

Katy walked very tentatively towards the table. There were more newspapers there than she had thought at first. An unnatural amount, in fact.

She looked at the page of the top one, read the caption and then placed her cup down on the table.

'Oh, no. Oh, no.' Her face drained of colour as she read the short piece. In a breezy, gossipy tone, it announced the engagement of one Katy West and one Bruno Giannella, who was glowingly described as easily the most eligible bachelor in London. With sickening, boot-licking flattery, the article sympathised with all those single females who were now to be deprived of a man lucky enough to be strikingly handsome, mouth-wateringly wealthy and too clever by half.

'That's my name,' Katy squeaked, sitting down heavily and then rifling through the selection of newspapers to find similar announcements in most of them. The *Financial Times* appeared to be the only one not to carry an article on the subject and who, she wondered frantically, ever read the *Financial Times* anyway?

'And Joseph…?'

'I felt I had to show him so that he could be spared finding it out through one of his friends. You know most of them probably only read the obituaries and the gossip.'

'Bruno, *this can't be happening*!'

'The evidence is in front of you.'

'How can you be so calm?' Katy shrieked with rising hysteria.

'I've had a bit more time to get used to it than you.' He swung round to face her and pulled his chair up towards the table. 'Isobel phoned me last night to inform me that I might be interested in having a look at the newspapers in the morning. By then, of course, it was too late for me to do anything about it. I came up here first thing.'

'My parents...' Katy went a shade more ashen. 'I...I have to call...tell them that it's all been a terrible mistake...' She looked across to the telephone and quailed at the thought of what would be involved. Her parents would demand an explanation of how such a rumour could occur in the first place. They would ask piercing questions, which she would be unable to answer. They would insist on driving up to make sure she was all right.

'What are we going to do?' she asked feverishly. 'You said that she wouldn't...'

'Seems she has an even more malicious streak than I imagined.'

'You have to sort this out!' Katy told him in a panicked voice. 'This is all your fault!'

'I wouldn't quite say *all mine*.'

'And the least you could do is *look a little more concerned*!' She couldn't sit down. She had to move around. She stood up, felt her legs want to give way and promptly sat back down. 'You have to make an announcement,' she continued, drawing in a big, shaky breath. 'Get in touch with your chums at…at the newspapers. You must have dozens of friends at the newspapers! Tell them they made a mistake. Explain about Isobel…' He was being very calm, she thought. And thank goodness for that, because two frantic people would have been even worse. She had a momentary pang of sympathy for him. He must be feeling just as frantic as she was, but, being a man of formidable self-control, he simply wasn't showing it. Right now, he probably loathed her for having unwittingly brought this appalling mess on his head.

'I'm sorry, Bruno,' Katy whispered. Tears were welling up and she blindly took the handkerchief that was shoved into her hand. 'I shouldn't have blamed you. If it hadn't been for me, none of this would have happened…' She rubbed her eyes fiercely with the hankie and then looked at him, still amazed that he could remain so *controlled*. But then Bruno was a highly disciplined man. He wouldn't burst into tears at something like this. He would probably have already thought it all through and come to a solution.

'I guess you've already thought of something…?' she asked hopefully.

'It's a bit too complicated for an easy solution,' he said, crushing any little glimmer of hope she had been nurturing.

'Too complicated? Surely you just have to tell them the truth…?'

'First of all, there's Joseph.' His brilliant black eyes locked hers and Katy felt herself getting giddy, then she remembered where getting giddy because of those fabulous eyes had got her, and she stared down at the crumpled hankie in her hand. 'He's over the moon about this development. It's put a real spring in his step. We've got to consider that he's just recovering from what could have been something a whole lot more serious. If we break it to him that these articles are all a lie, well…'

'You mean…he might have another heart attack?'

'Who knows? Probably not, but do we take the risk? Then there's your parents. If they haven't already read about it, then they will have by the end of the day. I don't know what they're like, but the picture I've got from you is of two very devoted, very caring people who would be deeply wounded to think that their only daughter had been…'

Katy, hanging onto every word leaving his lips, had no difficulty in picturing just how her poor, devoted parents would react. She swallowed back a stifled sob.

'And then there's my professional standing…'

'Your professional standing?' she parroted.

'I have a reputation in the City and, believe it or not, reputations are based on a whole lot more than just an ability to make money. Were I to be seen as a philanderer who leads a woman on, proposes marriage and then tries to wriggle out of the commitment, then what sort of man would I be seen as?'

'But you *are* a philanderer. Surely they know that already?'

Bruno's jaw clenched and he swallowed hard. 'I have enjoyed a bachelor life,' he muttered through gritted teeth. 'Which is quite different from having a fling with an innocent young girl, proposing marriage to her and then walking away.'

'They don't know that I'm young and innocent,' she whispered.

'They will, though. It won't be long before they head up here, cameras at the ready, to take pictures of the happy couple. My social life has always been followed.'

Katy didn't quite know which of these appalling options she should focus on. Joseph, her parents, Bruno's crumbling career and tarnished reputation or the press banging on the door to take pictures.

'It's awful,' she said in a small voice. 'What are we going to do?'

'I can only think of one thing,' he said in a low, thoughtful voice. He reached across the table and covered one of her hands with his. 'We're just going to have to pretend that the engagement is for real, that we're a happy couple…as far as the newspapers go, this is a flash in the pan. These stories have a very early sell-by date before they move on to something else.'

'And what about Joseph? My parents?'

'Trickier. We can't just carry it off for a few days and then stun them with the news that it was all a terrible mistake.'

'I suppose not,' Katy said, dazed.

'You should call your parents. If I'm to meet them, as I undoubtedly will, I don't want them arriving with low opinions of me. Bad enough, in their eyes, that I would have omitted to call them first and ask for your hand in marriage.'

'You're being very good about all this, Bruno. I realise you probably want to string me up from the nearest pole…' She became aware of the pressure of his hand on hers and hurriedly eased hers out. 'I'll call my parents.' It was a statement, not a question, and she knew she was rigid as a block of wood as she stumbled an explanation to her mother over the phone. Fifteen minutes later, she looked at Bruno with a forlorn expression.

'She thinks it's very romantic,' Katy said on a sigh. 'She said that she and Dad were engaged only a fort-night after they first met.' She sighed again. 'They're coming tomorrow. I couldn't stop them. They're dying to meet you.'

'Understandable.'

'They can stay in the local hotel. It's only half an hour's drive away.'

'I wouldn't dream of it and nor would Joseph. There's plenty of room here.'

'But…' How could she explain that having her parents here would be just too much? Taking the pretence too far? A quick meeting on neutral territory, and she was thinking of tea at the hotel, and there would be no time for them to form any real bonds. A couple of hours of polite chit-chat and then, when she announced that the engagement was over, that she and Bruno really didn't get along after all, they would accept it more easily.

She launched into a garbled explanation of her thinking and then waited until he shook his head slowly.

'It would seem inhospitable. Joseph, I know, would be mortified. He's nothing if not the soul of hospitality. He would enjoy nothing more than relaxing in the comfort of his own home with your parents, probably showing them his prized first editions and, of course, his orchids.'

Which was exactly what Katy feared. She opened her mouth to explain just that, but he interrupted her before she could begin,

'And besides, we shouldn't forget that he's still recovering from a fairly major health scare. He might seem to be forging ahead in the progress stakes, but anything could set him back and that includes an attack of nerves at having to meet your parents somewhere in town. I just think that he would be a lot happier if the meeting were to take place here.'

'You must be furious with me,' she said miserably.

'Don't worry about me. I can take care of myself.'

'Have you spoken to Isobel?'

'What would be the point? The thing is done now. We just have to work on sorting it out the best we can.'

'And how long do you think...?'

'Do I think what?'

'Well, how long do we have to go through with this charade?' His mouth tightened and Katy realised just how awful it would be for him. 'And what about your work?' Her frown eased and she nodded a little to herself. 'Oh, I understand what you're probably going to do. You're going to head back to London and then maybe commute on the weekends, and that way,' she said slowly, 'we can always say that things didn't work out because of your work commitments...' That scenario had a number of benefits, the most important being that if Bruno wasn't around, it would give her time to get her wayward heart in order.

'That's an option, indeed,' Bruno murmured noncommittally. He sat back and observed her flushed face.

Katy, conjuring up a scenario wherein she wasn't faced with the agony of being near him all the time, was nodding to herself. 'Yes, that's it. Maybe you could even *go somewhere. Travel* to another country where you would suddenly find yourself involved in a deal that took much, *much* longer than you'd expected. Days. Weeks! Of course, I would grow depressed and start wondering how we would be able to function as a married couple if you were going to be away for months on end. It would be only natural for our relationship to fizzle out, by which time Joseph and my parents would be braced for that to happen...'

'In the meantime,' he said with a depressing sense of purpose, dragging her full tilt right back into the reality she had been busily trying to avoid, 'we have to do something about a ring.'

'A ring?'

'An engagement ring. Joseph will expect you to be wearing one when he gets back from his little jaunt. If we leave now...' he looked at his watch and appeared to be making a few mental calculations '...we can be in town in half an hour.'

She had only sufficient time to grab her light jacket, ignoring the rumblings in her stomach, which had cottoned on to the fact that she had missed breakfast. She would have to grab something somewhere along the line. Or else eat as soon as they returned home.

An hour and a half later and after two jewellers who appeared to have nothing good enough for Bruno, she trailed behind him into the third jeweller's. As far as she was concerned, any ring would do. It was all a phoney engagement anyway, she told Bruno several times, so what did it matter what the ring looked like?

When a tray of impressive diamond rings was brought out for her to inspect, she cleared her throat and said in an ultra polite voice, 'Aren't these a bit *expensive*? For *what we have in mind*?'

'Nothing but the best for you,' Bruno murmured. He reached out and gently massaged the back of her neck with such intimacy that she felt her face going bright red.

Half an hour later, Katy was the recipient of a slender gold ring topped with two small diamonds. She had fallen in love with it. Choose something unappealing, she had sternly told herself as she had gazed down at the black velvet display board, and had immediately found her hand reaching out for the most charming engagement ring she had ever seen.

Now she couldn't help sneaking glances at her finger

and wondering what it would be like if this charade were reality, if Bruno really did love her.

'What's the loud sigh for?' he asked and Katy started.

'Did I sigh?'

She looked up at him, met his eyes and was busily thinking of something when he continued, 'I haven't got around to thanking you.' He pushed open the door to a coffee shop and Katy realised that somehow they had been walking in the direction of the town centre. She must have been miles away.

'You've done me a favour,' he drawled, ordering himself a black coffee and a café latte for her. She had a preference for the milky coffee. She could remember telling him that ages ago, though she was surprised that he had remembered. But then he *had* been cooped up with her for long enough. There had been none of the usual distractions that would have allowed such unnecessary information to filter out of his brain.

Bruno sat back and waited until his cup was deposited in front of him. 'There was no need for you to agree to this engagement. The pressure was entirely on me to account for myself.'

'Well, I still blame myself for getting you into the mess in the first place,' Katy mumbled. 'And I couldn't just walk away from it that easily. I mean, there was Joseph to consider and also my parents. They would have understood, but there would still have been some lingering doubts about what gave rise to such a revelation in the first place. No smoke without a fire sort of thing. Anyway, it's just for a little while, isn't it?'

'But, unfortunately, it might be slightly more hectic than we both initially imagined…at least to start with.'

'What do you mean?'

'I mean that it was a bit unrealistic to expect things to

remain in the closed circle of immediate friends and family. It's easy to think that it's possible to escape reality because Joseph lives in the countryside. Open fields lend the illusion of escape. Unfortunately, despite being a very private man, I happen to have a highly public profile. I've already received countless emails from business associates congratulating me and invitations for the both of us to make a public appearance at various gatherings.'

Katy visibly paled.

'Tomorrow night we've been jointly invited to a client do at the Royal Albert Hall.'

'But…that's *ridiculous*,' she squeaked.

'Be prepared for cameras.'

Katy gulped down several mouthfuls of latte and had a sickening feeling of being drawn into a web that was growing monstrously big and out of control.

'You'll have to find some excuse,' she said a little desperately.

'Such as?'

'I don't know! Use your imagination! I know we're in this mess now, but…'

'I'll limit the social engagements. In the meantime, I think it might be an idea if you expanded your wardrobe to cope with immediate eventualities.' He drained his coffee, sat back and folded his arms.

Katy could have hit him. He was so arrogant, so absolutely certain that he could control events. As far as he was concerned, they had agreed on a course of action and he would move with ruthless efficiency to implement it. No matter that she had feelings, no matter that she would be trailing along in his wake, waiting for him, no doubt, to decide when they could reasonably call the whole thing off after a decent interval. She would dress the part, play the part, and when the time was right she would have to walk away from the part as though it had never existed. He would never have imagined that this could cause her a problem. Why should it? It wouldn't cause him one. He would have walked away from her without a backward glance, but fate had thrown them together against his will and he would set about tackling the problem like he tackled everything else. Thoroughly.

'And what if I don't *want* my wardrobe expanded?'

Bruno shrugged. 'Up to you. The Royal Albert Hall is usually a fairly formal venue, though. If you don't think you would feel uncomfortable wearing what you wear here, those smocky type garments, to an event like that, then that's entirely up to you.'

'You are so *rude* and I *hate* the way you think you can manipulate people,' she whispered shakily under her breath.

'Is that how you see it?'

'I don't see why we can't just play this pretend game for a little while then let things fade away. No coming to London with you. No public appearances.'

'Just those reporters lurking in the bushes waiting for a candid shot. Trampling over the flowers. Driving Joseph into the house rather than face prying eyes peering at him through binoculars. There is nothing more juicy for a reporter, especially those of a paparazzi nature, than the whiff of the clandestine. They will see your refusal to be seen on my arm as an indication of something to hide. On the other hand, give them a few decent pictures and they'll soon disappear.'

'We shouldn't have started all this,' Katy said unsteadily.

'You mean we shouldn't have kissed one another by the pool that day? Or was the mistake in getting caught by a vengeful ex?'

'We should have just told the truth when we could have instead of…of…'

'No point going down the *should have* road. It always proves to be a very futile exercise.' Bruno stood up, dropped more than sufficient money to cover their coffees on the table and waited until Katy had reluctantly got to her feet.

How had she ever got so deep into this? It had seemed so easy at the time to evade the truth, with Joseph disappearing almost as soon as he had dropped his bombshell, and then Bruno using that silver tongue of his to make her follow his lead.

She barely noticed as they walked towards the town centre, nor did she pay the slightest bit of attention to the shop until they were standing inside it, at which point Katy blinked and hazarded a weak smile in Bruno's direction.

He had struck up a conversation with the proprietor. Katy was pretty sure that the woman would not have paid her the least attention had she come in on her own, but Bruno was the sort of man who exuded money. The tall, haughty brunette's nose seemed to visibly twitch as she conversed with him, pointing out new collections and sparing Katy one brief, speculative glance that spoke volumes.

When Bruno insinuated that a buying spree was imminent, Katy took a deep breath and said very firmly, 'One outfit. One social occasion, one outfit.'

To her surprise, he smiled and moved over to where she was standing resolutely by the door. 'And here I was, thinking that women loved having things bought for them,' he murmured.

'Don't stand so close to me,' Katy hissed.

'We're engaged. Remember? Engaged people have a

tendency to stand close to one another. It's almost expected. Anyway, you'll have to get used to it. Your parents and Joseph might be a bit alarmed if we spend the evening on opposite sides of the room.'

'Well I don't see Joseph *or* my parents around at the moment, do you? Just one very snobbish sales assistant who doesn't know us from Adam.'

'No point doing a job unless you do it properly,' was his response.

So now she was reduced to the status of a job that needed to be done. She shouldn't be surprised considering Isobel had been little more than a suitable possible arrangement at the time, but it still made her feel sick inside to know just how disposable she was. And she really wished he would move away. Her body had a memory and a will of its own and his proximity was making her burn with something that was definitely not dislike.

He must have read her mind because he sauntered off and sat down on the chair located at the side of the room, for a bird's-eye view of assessing various outfits.

'Right,' he drawled, the object of what Katy could only call slavering attention from the sales assistant, 'a few casual pieces, no ridiculous styles, and one dressy outfit suitable for mixing with royalty.'

Katy scooted over to the chair and fixed him with a glare. 'I realise that I'm nothing more than a *job number*,' she muttered, 'but isn't this taking things a bit too far? Have you any idea how much these clothes cost? And I won't be able to use them and return them for a refund. You'll be throwing an awful lot of money down the drain when the *job* is finished and you have the clothes back.'

Bruno's mouth thinned and he looked at her coldly. 'I find that remark particularly tasteless,' he said, but, instead of being squashed by the iciness of his voice and the patent anger burning in his black eyes, Katy felt a little swoop of delight that she had managed to somehow get behind the indifference and prod him into a reaction. It hadn't seemed fair that *she* should be so churned up by this horrible complication, so gutted by her own emotions, while he remained so composed, controlled and infuriatingly unmoved.

'But it's the truth,' she insisted with wide-eyed, bemused innocence. More satisfaction as his face darkened. 'Once the job's finished, all of this will just be money wasted.'

'You can keep the damn clothes,' Bruno muttered harshly, 'and the ring for that matter. Forget about the money.'

'I certainly would never dream of keeping either, especially the ring.' She twisted it self-consciously on her slender finger. 'An engagement ring should mean something and this ring doesn't mean anything at all. When I wear an engagement ring for keeps, it'll be because it's cementing a worthwhile relationship and not...not something like this.'

Bruno's jaw hardened and he stared stonily at her. 'I think the sales assistant is getting a little restless,' he remarked with pointed patience. 'And this conversation is going nowhere. If you decide you don't want to keep the clothes, then they'll be given to charity.' He looked away from her, folded his legs and gave the sales assistant an imperceptible nod.

The brunette's cue to move into immediate action.

Of course, she wouldn't *keep* the clothes. They weren't her style *at all*. And of course, despite their one night of passion, she had made no emotional impact on him, quite a different story for her with her gullible heart and foolish longings. But...

If this was play-acting, then why not obey the decree he had laid down and enter into the spirit of it? She stilled the little voice whispering in her ear that maybe, just maybe, she could show him that she wasn't the *smock dress* country bumpkin he labelled her, that she could look sexy if she wanted.

Having never done it before, Katy was bemused to find that the process was more enjoyable and a lot easier than she had imagined. She tried on outfits, she twirled, she marvelled at how the cut of the clothes made her figure look like a figure instead of the off-putting boyish build she had always thought she possessed.

Bruno, gallingly, made no flattering noises, and while Katy tried to ignore the aching disappointment in her heart, she couldn't help feeling hurt that he limited his remarks to the essential, and when the trying-on was over simply got to his feet, instructed the sales assistant to deliver the lot to the house by mid afternoon and paid the bill.

The hurt developed a wall of icy protectiveness over it and as they left the shop she turned to him brightly.

'I've changed my mind.'

'What about?' Bruno asked, not looking at her and showing marginal interest.

'About the clothes. You can have back the ring but maybe I'll keep the clothes...' She slid him a sidelong glance, hating herself for just wanting him so much to compliment her on how she had looked. 'After all,' she tacked on casually, 'once this is over and done with, they might come in very handy when it comes to meeting guys. You were right all along. I can't bury myself up here any longer. Course, I'll still work with Joseph but…well…there's a whole world waiting out there, isn't there…?'

CHAPTER NINE

KATY lay down on the bed and stared up at the ceiling. There wasn't much to see. It was after midnight, she hadn't bothered to switch the lights on and only the moonshine filtering through the curtains picked out the contours of the room.

She couldn't quite decide what tonight had been: raging success or abysmal failure.

Her parents had arrived at teatime and had been, unsurprisingly, a little taken aback at the size of the house and the gardens. Katy had been overjoyed to see them. She phoned regularly, but only managed to make it to her home town at irregular intervals and seeing them in her own surroundings had been wonderful. She had shown them around the house, strolled through the gardens, chatted when she'd had to about Bruno in a vague and hopefully contented voice, by which time they had relaxed and then Joseph had appeared, apologetic about not having been there to greet them,

'But an old man with a tired heart apparently needs to rest fifty per cent of the day,' he confided with an impish glint in his eyes, at which point all ice melted.

There was a little window during which no searchingly intrusive questions were asked and Bruno, tangled up in a three-hour conference call to America, had not yet appeared.

They took tea outside; her mother chatted animatedly about Joseph's orchids. Naturally, it couldn't have lasted. By the time Bruno surfaced, her mother had cornered her

and the catalogue of questions had begun. Interested, concerned, a little too shrewd. Then her father had cornered
her, ostensibly to apologise for her mother being a little
too much of an inquisitor but really so that he could
reassure himself that his little girl was not making the
biggest mistake of her life.

Who was this Bruno character? Why the speed? Had
they had time to get to know one another? What sort of
man was he? Was he a family type of man? When were
they planning on getting married?

Then, when Joseph tactfully excused himself so that
he could chat to Maggie about dinner preparations, she
was subjected to a dual attack.

By the time Bruno emerged from the office, Katy was
feeling drained and hunted.

She had hoped to waylay him so that she could make
her case for treading carefully and avoiding too many
detailed answers that might come back to haunt them
when the unravelling of their so-called relationship began. She had also, subconsciously, wanted him to sym-
pathise with her in the face of all the parental questions
she had had to fend, but in all events he was in a foul
mood.

No one else was able to glimpse that. He had enough
surface charm to bowl anyone over and her parents were
no exception. He played the part of the perfect gentleman. He was amusing, asked countless questions about
them, made fluent conversation on topics her father was
interested in and he was aggravatingly solicitous in his
dealings with her.

Intimate looks, a hand circling her waist, a swift kiss
on the nape of her neck. She felt every touch and her
body responded with savage enthusiasm, all the worse
because of his foul mood, which she had spotted. How

could he pretend so successfully when he was simmering over something? Probably the conference call?

The whole show had made her see just how much she had bitten off. She fell into an unsatisfactory sleep two hours later and woke up to bright sunlight bathing the room because she had forgotten to close the curtains.

Resolve was what was called for, she told herself, getting dressed in one of her new, startling outfits, which was a figure-hugging beige top and the same style loose, calf-length skirt she was accustomed to wearing, but this time one that sat on her hips, revealing a slither of firm stomach and her belly button.

Resolve and a bit of damage limitation. She couldn't let her parents go away in the false hope that a marriage date would be set by the time she next got in touch.

Ready for anything, Katy arrived downstairs to find that she had timed her entrance perfectly. All the assembled cast were there. Maggie had prepared a buffet-style breakfast in the dining room and, after a few pleasantries, she sat down and prepared to launch phase one of her plan.

'I'm surprised you're not off to work, *darling*.' She glanced over to where Bruno was sitting opposite her and Joseph, sandwiched between her parents.

Having failed to dredge up the slightest compliment when she had been in the designer shop, parading herself in various outfits, he had, she noticed sourly, managed to tell her that she looked exquisite when she had appeared in the dining room, and had sounded as though he had meant every word. Her parents and Joseph had shared a look of mutual pleasure. She, on the other hand, had seen it for what it was. More play-acting. As were the searing glances he had thrown her way and the kiss he had planted on her lips. It all went a long way to making her feel more determined to curtail any rising expectations.

'Day off,' Bruno drawled now, looking up at her and managing to lock the rest of the room out so that she felt annoyingly red-faced.

'Mmm.' Katy sighed and gave everyone a slight smile. 'Unusual. Bruno is *such* a hard worker. Aren't you?'

'Works like the devil,' Joseph obligingly chipped in. 'Always has. Can't tell you how many countries he visits in a year.'

'Hundreds, I imagine!' Katy took up the thread before Bruno could jump in with amusing anecdotes about the places he had visited. She could already see interest hovering on her father's lips.

'Not quite.' Bruno closed his knife and fork and looked at her with brooding speculation.

'Where have you been?' her mother joined in. 'Anywhere exciting?' Whereupon Bruno turned to her and wittily described some of the places he had visited, the customs he had come across, the weird food he had had to sample. All the time Katy could feel his dark interest levelled on her and, sure enough, the minute the gathering broke up, with her parents excusing themselves so that they could pack for their homeward journey, he managed to corner her.

'What was that all about?'

'What was what all about?'

'You know what I'm talking about, Katy. The sudden fascination with the many hundreds of countries I travel to in a year.'

Katy shrugged. 'I just thought we should start building up the scene for our eventual incompatibility. At the rate you're going, everyone's going to start asking us for wedding dates next and then what? Better to sow a few seeds of doubt.' His face was looking grimmer by the minute but Katy was not going to be deterred.

'Mum and Dad will probably have a cup of tea before I drop them to the station and I think you ought to imply how inconvenient you've found it being here for weeks on end, in one place. Maybe you could say that your work suffered because you need to be travelling around, *touching base*, with all those companies or whatever that you own.'

'Progress a lie with another, in other words.'

'But a *helpful* lie!' Their conversation was taking place in the sitting room. Katy could hear the distant clatter of Maggie clearing away the breakfast dishes. In a minute, her parents would come in and so would Joseph. She felt an overwhelming desperation to get something sorted out before they entered. 'I know my mum,' Katy said urgently, perching against the bay window sill, which meant that she had to crane her neck upwards to look at Bruno. 'I don't know how you've done it, but you've managed to convince her that you're the perfect son-in-law-to-be. No, I take that back. I *know* how you did it. You're such an expert liar and you just don't have any moral standards, do you?'

Bruno leaned down towards her and rested the palms of his hands on either side of her, caging her in.

'We went into this together. It's no good trying to lay the blame at my door now.'

'Okay, so I made a mistake. I can begin to rectify that now, though, by not encouraging Mum and Dad to start thinking that this is actually going somewhere. All I need is a bit of co-operation from you!'

'Why the sudden sense of urgency here, Katy?' Bruno enquired coldly. 'There's been no mention of any wedding date.'

'That's not the point. Anyway, it's just not been mentioned *at the moment*. They've come here to check you out and, now that you've passed muster, it *won't be long* before I start getting little suggestions about wedding invitations and churches and bridal dresses.' Katy shuddered at the possibility that this charade could carry on for that length of time, the thought that she would have to continue seeing Bruno, being in his presence, going out with him, having him touch her whenever the situation demanded a show of some affection, knowing that the touch meant nothing to him but meant everything to her. Every second in his presence gave her love time to grow and dragged her further into the net she could feel tangling around her.

She could feel his warm breath fanning her face, could feel the nearness of him like some dreadful fever against which her immune system was defenceless. Every nerve ending in her body was alive with the treacherous excitement induced by his powerful masculine presence.

'My parents are old-fashioned kind of people,' she carried on desperately. 'They won't see the point of a so-called engagement unless a date is set for the big event! And Joseph probably won't either. I know he's been brilliant getting back on his feet, but he still feels vulnerable. He might think that time is no longer on his side and his godson should tie the knot sooner rather than later. Have you considered that?' She shot him an attacking glance from under her lashes and watched his face suffuse with dark colour.

'I'm in the process of considering a lot of things, as a matter of fact.'

There was an iciness in his voice that sent a little shiver racing down her spine.

'Would any of those things be what I was just talking

about?' Katy asked nervously. The closer she had got with Bruno, the less nervous she had begun to feel around him, but right now the forbidding cast to his features had her heart pumping like a wild, trapped bird inside her.

'I would say that I'm making a connection here between what you said yesterday and what you're telling me now...'

'What? What did I say yesterday?' Katy frowned and tried to think back but, since she had no idea what he was on about, it was impossible to isolate any strands of conversation that might have given her some clues as to where he was heading.

'The clothes. The clothes that you've now decided to keep because you've suddenly realised that they might just come in handy. Oh, yes. The shy, stammering girl of the printed floral smock has taken stock and seen that a wardrobe of classy clothes can go a long way to trapping a man. Didn't you say so yourself? And why wait before you put it to the test? Mmm? I can see why this' pretend engagement is getting on your nerves all of a sudden...'

'You can have your clothes back!'

'What's it like taking the leap from innocent young girl to woman on the prowl, Katy?' He looked at her flushed face and the thought of her going out into that deadbeat town, shimmying her slender hips and giving men that unknowingly sexy look of provocative innocence, exploded in his head like a fistful of fireworks. He felt the unexpected rage of a jealousy he had never experienced before and didn't know what to do with.

'You gave a very convincing performance of a timid young thing scared at the prospect of losing her virginity. Now I think about it, were you really that scared? Who knows? Maybe you had plans...is that it, Katy? Did you have plans to use me? After all, you have to admit that I'm a supremely good catch...'

'Plans to use you? What was I planning to use you for?'

Bruno overrode her question savagely. 'You're twenty-three. Maybe, just maybe you decided that it was high time you lost your virginity and who better than a single man with money? Lots of it? With Isobel out of the way, you'd have no need for any conscience...' Staring down into her startled, bewildered eyes, he knew that he was being utterly implausible. He was attacking, losing control and his loss of control was driving him crazy. He couldn't rid himself of the image of her laughing with some other man, sending him those shy little looks that she had sent to him, taking her clothes off, getting into bed...

He pushed himself away from her and fought to regain his self composure.

'I don't know what you're on about.' Katy restlessly twisted her fingers together and finally walked over to where he had subsided onto one of the sofas. 'I'm not after anything from you,' she said miserably. 'I don't understand how you can make a series of connections like you have and come up with all the wrong answers. We just happen to have found ourselves in an odd situation. I mean, if it weren't for Isobel and her need to get revenge we wouldn't even *be* here!' He would have been on his way to some other woman's bed, she thought to herself, because she wouldn't conduct a casual fling with him, and she might have been recovering from the body-blow he had delivered to her instead of being catapulted on a roller-coaster ride for a variety of reasons that were growing less convincing by the second.

'No, we damn well wouldn't,' Bruno said grimly.

'But we are and we can hardly wriggle out of it from day one.'

'I object to you telling me that I'm some kind of opportunist.' Katy felt the need to clear the air. 'I didn't plan to lose...well, to make love to you...it just happened, and I don't care how much money you have or not. That's appalling. I would *never* enter into a relationship because of money. That's a really unfair accusation.' She could feel tears struggling to well up and fought them back. Bursting into tears would infuriate Bruno. After all, he hadn't asked for this mess to land on his head either and, whatever she thought now about the situation they had found themselves in, and the rights and wrongs of it, the plain truth was that they had entered into it for the right reasons.

'Okay. I apologise,' Bruno said, flushing darkly.

His apology only made her want to cry more. Katy gulped, feeling emotional, and with a frustrated sigh Bruno leaned towards her and pulled her into him. His hands tangled in her hair and, like a blind man, he sought her mouth with his, parting her lips with hungry ferocity and plundering the soft moistness.

He could feel the softness of her small breasts squashing against his chest and with a moan he pushed his hands underneath her shirt and pulled down the nothing of her stretchy cotton bra so that her breasts popped out of their restraints.

'What...are...you...doing?' Katy whispered shakily. His big hands covered her breasts and she shuddered with exquisite, agonised pleasure in response as his thumbs rubbed her nipples until she wanted to scream out with longing.

'What are *we* doing, you mean...'

'You shouldn't be touching me like this…it's not part of the deal…'

'Then why are you responding?' He pushed up the shirt so that he could look at what he was doing and breathed thickly as he saw the evidence of her arousal. Nipples big and dark, the buds tightly begging him to continue doing what he was doing. 'I want to suck them,' he groaned softly. 'Do you want that?'

'I want…' She knew what she wanted. Or at least, she thought she did. She wanted him to put distance between them, she wanted to step back from feelings that had taken control of her and were holding her common sense to ransom. Katy gazed deep into his bright black eyes and the protests died in her throat. Instead of pulling back and putting her case forward for not touching her again, she arched up slightly so that one breast dipped tantalisingly against his mouth.

The touch of his wet tongue against her sensitised nipple was almost unbearably exciting. He delicately licked the bud, then, when he could stand it no longer, Bruno pulled her down so that he could ravage her breast with his mouth, suckling at it and blindingly aroused by her responses.

They both heard the sound of approaching footsteps and voices and Katy shot off him and frantically got herself in order just as her parents walked into the sitting room. Packed and ready to go, they said. Joseph had offered to have Jimbo drop them off at the station, and that, her mum continued, taking in her daughter's flushed face with knowing eyes, seemed like a good idea, especially as Katy and Bruno would be going out later.

It seemed like a very good idea to Katy as well. Normally, she would have enjoyed the trip to the station and the cup of tea while they waited for the train, but this time she had a pretty shrewd idea of what being cooped up with her parents might involve.

So there had been no mention of a wedding date. *Yet.* But her mother had given her a very perceptive look when she had walked into the sitting room, only just missing catching them *in flagrante.*

She and Bruno and Joseph saw them off, standing on the drive. Bruno, true to form, had his hand circling her waist, although as soon as the Range Rover had disappeared from sight and Joseph was inside the house Katy edged her way out of the embrace.

She couldn't bring herself to look at him, although she was keenly aware of him next to her, not saying a word, hands stuck into his pockets. It was the perfect early-summer morning, quite still and very quiet, which had always been one of the most appealing things about the location of Joseph's house. No sounds of traffic or trains or overhead planes to intrude on the littler noises of the breeze through the trees and the birds singing.

It seemed hypocritical to launch into a speech about sticking to the deal and only doing what was necessary for just as long as it was necessary, when only a short while earlier she had been lying in his arms offering herself to him like the proverbial sacrificial lamb.

'What time do we need to leave this afternoon?' she asked in a detached voice, keeping her distance and still not looking at him. Instead she inspected the gravelley stones at her feet, kicking them slightly with the toe of her shoe.

'The car comes at five-thirty. Just spit it out.'

Katy raised her eyes to his and blushed.

'This evening will be a complete fiasco if you go into one of your thoughtful, silent moods so I suggest you just tell me what's on your mind and get it out into the open.'

'You know what I'm thinking.' By 'complete fiasco' she wondered if he meant that she would simply irritate the hell out of him if she wasn't prepared to conduct an Oscar-winning performance of a woman in love for the benefit of the public at large.

'You're beating yourself up because we touched one another. Am I right?'

Katy nodded and folded her arms.

'Well, I won't waste my time trying to talk you out of your over-developed guilt complex,' Bruno drawled, looking at her with an inscrutable expression, 'so let's just put the blame solidly on my shoulders. If my memory serves me right, I yanked you down on top of me and started kissing you. It won't happen again.'

'It won't?' For some reason, his ready assurance was woefully disappointing, but Katy managed to rally round with something she hoped resembled intense relief.

'It won't.'

'You mean because you don't fancy me any more.'

Bruno gave her a crooked smile but maintained a respectful distance. 'I never said that, did I? I just won't lay a finger on you if the aftermath is anguish on your part. Of course, that's not to say that I won't ravish you if you decide to make the first move.'

Disappointment gave way to foolish rapture, then she reminded herself of the million and one downsides to the offer he was extending.

'Well, I won't,' Katy said shortly. 'It would be stupid and short-sighted.' She thought of sleeping with him, again and again and again, without getting tied up in emotional knots and thinking about the future they would never have together. She thought about being carefree enough to just enjoy the moment. She wondered how it would be if she broke her own rules.

Before she could let herself speculate out loud on any of this, she began moving back into the house, aware of him right there behind her.

'Shall I meet you in the hall, then? At five-thirty?' she suggested.

'Feel better after our little chat?'

Katy shrugged. 'I'll feel better when tonight's over. When,' she asked suddenly, 'are you going to go back to London, Bruno? I can't imagine you can stay trapped up here indefinitely, even if there's a fake engagement to keep in motion for a while.'

Bruno's eyes narrowed and he looked at her thoughtfully. 'I'll work something out. I've got to go out to the town right now, so I won't be around for lunch.'

'Where are you going?' Katy blurted out, without thinking first, and then reddened.

'I have a clandestine meeting with a hot blonde,' he said lazily, his stunning eyes intent on her face.

Katy's mouth parted in shocked confusion. It took her a few seconds to realise that he was teasing her and then she glared at him.

'Very funny.'

'Jealous?'

'Certainly not! You're free to do exactly what you like.'

'Even though we're engaged?' Bruno shook his head sorrowfully. 'Don't you think I have *any* principles at all?'

'We're *not engaged* and I'm sure you haven't got any principles at all.'

His eyes hardened fractionally. 'This could really lead to an involved conversation, which I don't have the time for right now. The hot blonde is, in fact, a fifty-something lawyer in town who's handling something for me up here.'

'Okay.' Katy had the uneasy feeling that she had been foolish, accusing him of having no principles. She wanted to apologise, but didn't quite know how and, besides, she could see that he was itching to be off. He had already glanced at his watch twice.

When they touched each other he became a different person. She could almost believe that he felt something for her, could almost kid herself that a man couldn't possibly be so passionate about a woman he felt nothing for. But at times like this, standing five feet away from her with other things on his mind, it was as though that other side of him was all just an illusion.

This was why she knew that she could never cave in and enter into the loveless but sexually fulfilling relationship he seemed to want. Because brief, passionate bouts of togetherness in a bed could never compensate for the confused isolation she felt when he withdrew from her.

Tonight, she thought later as she got dressed for an event she had no desire to attend…tonight she would talk to him seriously about what they had to do to deal with this awkward situation. She just couldn't cope with it. She couldn't cope with knowing that he physically wanted her and would be willing to indulge in some casual sex for a while; she couldn't cope with resisting him even though she knew that that was what she had to do; she couldn't cope with being around him and pretending, without knowing when the pretence would end.

He would have to come up with some practical solutions, she decided, taking her time with her make-up for fear of ending up looking like an overdone B-list actress on a bad day. Or else she would pull the plug. There would be disappointment on Joseph's part and on her parents', but disappointment would fade over time.

By five-fifteen she was ready and she stood up to inspect herself in the mirror.

What stared back at her was nothing short of a complete transformation.

Her modest height had been boosted by a good three inches, thanks to some very delicate cream open toed sandals. Her slimness no longer looked unwomanly, but elegant, with her cream calf-length dress clinging fashionably to her waist and bust and revealing slender shoulders and the hint of a cleavage, which had been cleverly enhanced by her bra. She had swept up her hair, something she rarely did because it was just so much trouble trying to restrain it with clips, and tendrils curled around her face. Her eyes looked enormous.

Joseph, with a wicked glint in his eyes, further boosted her ego with lavish compliments and veiled remarks about hoping they made it to London because Bruno might just find her too tempting to last the journey.

'Unlikely,' Katy remarked, 'with a chauffeur in the front. What would he do with him? Stick him in the boot?' She worriedly wondered how Joseph would react when he found out that they were no longer an engaged couple.

She was still sunk in her reverie when she emerged onto the landing at five-thirty and the first she saw of Bruno were his shoes. Handmade, black patent leather. Her eyes travelled slowly upwards, taking in his formal DJ, all black aside from the pristine white shirt, punctuated by a black bow-tie.

'Wow,' she gasped and he raised his eyebrows in amusement.

'Ditto.'

He looked fabulous. He always looked fabulous. Now, however, in his supremely formal wear, he made her mouth run dry.

'Yes, you *shall* go to the ball,' he drawled, extending his elbow so that she linked her arm through it.

'And what when midnight strikes?' Katy asked lightly, thinking of the cold wall of reality waiting for them just around the corner. In fact, probably around midnight, when the ball was over and she sat down with Bruno to tell him what she knew she had to.

'Make sure you leave your sandal behind so that I can follow the trail.'

Nothing had prepared her for the fuss of their arrival at the Royal Albert Hall. The drive down to London had been passed in relative harmony. They had been the perfect example of two people making sure not to tread on any delicate subjects. She, because she was saving up her uncomfortable speech for later, and he, she assumed, because anything too taxing in the back of a car would irritate him and possibly ruin what he anticipated being a public canvas of their united togetherness.

She had managed to convince herself that it might just be feasible to slink into the hall, unnoticed by too many people.

She hadn't banked on the photographers waiting as cars pitched up, disgorging their passengers. She stepped out of the chauffeured car to the glare of cameras flashing and the press of journalists jostling for the best shot from behind a cordon.

Instinctively she reached out and slipped her hand into Bruno's, calming down when he responded with a warm squeeze that was just the right gesture to make her feel a bit more at ease, and she was more than willing to let her hand remain there even after they had walked the plank and finally entered the impressive building.

Bruno Giannella was, she began acknowledging faintly, a bigger deal than she had ever anticipated. He was recognised by countless people, hailed out and spoken to with deference. He was a presence that many, she was fast realising, were inclined to court. And since she came as part of the bargain, they were obsequiously polite to her as well. Katy doubted any of them would have even turned to glance at her under any other circumstances. No wonder he was so keen on maintaining appearances, on not being seen as a cad in any way, shape or form.

'I never realised that you were so...*important*...' she whispered, when they were finally seated.

Bruno, his arm on the rest between them, leaned into her. 'Would you have behaved differently?' he asked with some interest, turning to look at her.

'Of course I would have! I would have tried even harder to avoid you whenever you came to visit Joseph!' Her breath caught in her throat at the smile of pure amusement that lit up his face.

'I wonder why I believe every word of that...' he murmured, looking away as the lights dimmed and the orchestra began to play.

Everything about the night was magical and impressive. The crowd thronged with recognisable, celebrity faces. The performance was glorious. It all added up to a spectacle that Katy knew she would do well to commit to memory, as it would never again be repeated.

She almost felt like a traitor, she sighed to Bruno when the evening had finally come to an end and everyone was trooping out to claim their expensive, chauffeur-driven cars.

'Why do I think that this is about to lead to some nonsense remark about not being good enough to be here?'

'Well…' Katy glanced around her at the beautiful people in their immaculate designer clothing '…because it happens to be true, I suppose.'

'You're far better than most of the people here,' he said in a matter-of-fact voice. 'What you're looking at are expensive trappings.' He shrugged and cast a scornful glance around him. 'In the end, they count for nothing.'

'I know you're just saying that to make me feel better,' Katy told him, loving him so much that it hurt, 'but thanks anyway.' She smiled up at him, barely feeling the coolness of the night air on her arms and hardly aware of the remaining photographers still lurking around for possible last-minute shots.

She certainly wasn't aware of a tall blonde woman moving towards them, with a tall fair-haired man glued to her side.

In fact Katy only noticed Isobel's presence when the familiar cut-glass voice broke through the blissful moment to offer congratulations to the happy couple.

Katy blinked to find Isobel staring at her with hard, satisfied eyes but, before she had time to open her mouth, Bruno was responding with unhurried, lethal coolness, accepting the congratulations for all the world as though they were sincerely meant, smiling as he informed the blonde that breaking up with her had been the best thing he had ever done.

A look of pure rage crossed Isobel's face and she shrugged off the restraining hand her companion had placed on her. 'Oh, really. I know you well enough to know that this so-called engagement has been forced on you.' She laughed. 'Couldn't be seen to be a conscience-free womaniser with some little halfwit from the back of nowhere, could you? A man in your position?'

Katy felt the simmering violence surging through Bruno, although when he spoke his voice was perfectly controlled.

'You couldn't be more wrong, my dear. This engagement is entirely for real...'

'So you wouldn't mind setting a date?'

'Not in the slightest.' He signalled to one of the lurking photographers with a nod and then, while Katy watched with open-mouthed amazement, said with absolute assurance and in a voice that was meant to be heard by anyone interested enough to listen and within earshot, 'Just to let you boys know that you'll be cordially invited to cover my wedding to...' he raised Katy's hand to his lips and brushed his mouth against it '...this exquisite creature within the next month. We'll be finalising details before the end of the week.' Several more photographers had shot across for the announcement. The last glimpse Katy had of them was as they took rapid pictures of her before Bruno bent down and covered her mouth with his in a searingly passionate kiss.

CHAPTER TEN

SHOCK carried Katy through the next five minutes. She had little fleeting snapshots in her head of reporters lapping up the surprise announcement and firing questions at them, which Bruno fielded with his usual grace, of Isobel fading away into the background, of Bruno's darkly handsome face staring down at her before leading her to the car that had been waiting for them.

She only realised she was trembling when the car door was slammed and the car pulled away from the kerb, then she turned slowly to Bruno, who was watching her intently, his eyes guarded.

'I think I just had a bad dream,' was all she could find to say.

'No dream.' The car was equipped with a sliding screen that protected the confidentiality of conversations being carried out in the back seat. 'Just keep driving, Harry, until I tell you to stop.'

'Where to, sir?'

'Wherever the hell you want. Brighton and back for all I care.' He slid shut the glass partition and then drew a discreet navy curtain so that they were now ensured total privacy.

'Please tell me that what I think happened didn't happen at all,' Katy pleaded, kicking off the super-high sandals and tucking one foot under her as she swivelled in the seat to face him.

'I can't do that.'

'*Do you realise what you've gone and done?*' He

178

looked so damn calm that she could have hit him. 'How could you? *How could you?*'

Bruno looked at her and seemed to be contemplating something. Right now, though, Katy wasn't too curious as to what that something might be. She just knew that the man sitting next to her, within touching distance, had committed them both to a course of action from which escape was going to be nigh on impossible.

'Don't get hysterical,' he ordered calmly, at which point Katy's hysteria went up a few more notches.

'Don't get *hysterical*? How am I supposed to get, Bruno? Oh, good heavens.' She buried her head in the palm of her hand and closed her eyes tightly shut for a few seconds. 'How are we ever going to get out of this one? It was bad enough with the engagement but at least that was something we could call off. But *marriage*? No, we're not married yet. We won't have to actually *get out of a marriage*. We'll just have to sort of hope that people somehow forget what you said. Yes, that's it. In a month's time, no one will remember anything about a wedding date being set.' She cast her mind back to the attention he had had focused on him, the sheer number of people he seemed to know, the interest the reporters had taken in him even though there had been dozens of other famous people arriving for the do. She felt her heart sink. Tomorrow the tabloids would gleefully announce his ridiculous remark about them getting married within the month and her parents and Joseph would be the first on the phone to shriek their congratulations. Her parents would be alarmed that she hadn't spoken with them first about the date, but that would be forgotten in the face of the joy at seeing their little baby tie the knot.

Katy groaned at the seeming inevitability of it all.

'How could you let that woman goad you into saying what you said, Bruno? How could you?'

'It would be inconceivable that anyone could goad me into doing anything,' Bruno said quietly, his face flushing, but Katy was miles away with a metaphorical net getting tighter and tighter around her.

'Only this morning we were planning how we could start letting Joseph and my parents down gently and now…' The enormity of what that 'now' consisted of was so mind-boggling that for a few seconds she was lost for words. Her eyes glazed over and she stared past Bruno into an imaginary not-too-distant future in which a heart-broken Joseph and two disillusioned parents played starring roles.

'I suppose you're waiting for an apology,' Bruno remarked in a clipped voice and Katy's attention snapped back into focus. She looked at him with incredulity.

'Apology? Why would I want an apology? I'd much rather have an explanation! We've just jumped straight out of a frying-pan into a fire, Bruno!'

'Have we?'

'You know we have!' She watched as he turned away from her so that he could fold his hands behind his head, his stunning dark eyes firmly fixed on the curtained-off partition in front of him.

'Why?' he asked in a barely audible voice and Katy strained towards him, wondering whether she had heard correctly.

'What do you mean?' she asked, bewildered. If she hadn't known better, she would have suspected that Bruno had had too much to drink and was rambling.

The silence hung between them, heavy with unspoken undertones that she couldn't quite manage to decipher.

'We're engaged. Well, why shouldn't we get married?'

The suggestion was so absolutely shocking that she sucked in a mouthful of air like someone gasping for oxygen.

'I mean,' Bruno carried on, still not looking at her, 'you can't say that we don't get along and we're physically attracted to one another. Sex is a very important aspect of a successful marriage, you know. Good sex and an ability to get along. And, face it, Joseph and your parents would be very happy with the situation.'

It took a few moments before the penny dropped and she realised where he was going. Without emotional involvement, Bruno might well see marrying her as an acceptable conclusion to the farce they had stupidly instigated. After all, hadn't he himself told her at one point that he thought it might be a good time to settle down? Isobel had been considered for the position but she hadn't worked out. Now, here they were, in the perfect situation to move seamlessly from a phoney engagement into a loveless but highly convenient marriage, and one which he knew would fulfil the highly essential criterion of pleasing his godfather. As he said, he was attracted to her and he liked her well enough. Any concept of love wouldn't have featured in his equation because as far as he was concerned love simply didn't exist.

A tide of hot colour surged into her cheeks and she felt the brutal spark of anger stir inside her.

'You used to tell me that I irritated you when I didn't look at you when addressed,' she snapped, pushed into a display of behaviour she would never have thought herself capable of, 'so I'd be really grateful if you could look at me now!'

He obliged and the shift in his body weight brought them a few inches more dangerously close together.

'Has it occurred to you *at all* that I might not share

your…your wonderfully romantic notions about what constitutes a perfect marriage?' Katy clenched her hands into two fists. 'Believe it or not, I don't *want* to walk down the aisle to say I *do* to a man who kind of likes me and at the moment is physically attracted to me! Though, the physical attraction side of things might come to an end at any given moment in time! I don't *want* to get married because you happen to think it's convenient and various relatives might quite like it if we did! How can you be so *arrogant* and *conceited* to imagine that I'd fall in with your plans! I'm not Isobel, you know!'

'I know,' Bruno said softly, which was enough to momentarily throw her off balance, though not for long once she started thinking about it again. 'You're nothing like Isobel,' he continued in the same disconcerting voice. 'And you're nothing like any of the women I've ever dated in my life before. You're unique. I never really knew how unique until I started spending time in your company and I got accustomed to the way you thought and spoke and smiled.'

'You can't butter me up into going along with your idiotic plans,' Katy whispered, but his words were having a decidedly pleasurable effect on her nervous system.

'I'm not trying to butter you up. I'm just telling you the truth.' He reached out to brush the back of his hand across her flushed cheek and she had to control the urge to leap straight at him and bury herself against him. 'I've spent all of my adult life dating women who knew the right words and the right clothes for any occasion. When Joseph became ill and I had to go up to the country to stay, I thought that being around someone as nervous as you always seemed to be would drive me round the bend. I was wrong. I kind of started feeling as though I'd been swept off on some magical mystery tour and I liked the feeling.'

Katy tried not to like the feeling his silvered words were doing to her too much.

'I found myself wondering what you looked like...'

'What I looked like?'

'Underneath your camouflage clothes,' he observed succinctly and she blushed at the candour.

'Part of the reason I imported Isobel was to ward off the wicked thoughts I was beginning to have about you. In a way, it was the best thing I ever did because just seeing her next to you convinced me that she was all wrong for me.'

Katy drew in a deep, shaky breath. 'Which isn't to say that I'm right for you,' she said. 'Okay, you like me. I'm not the complete awkward idiot you thought I was going to be.' She frowned and was distracted by the glaring truth that she was, in fact, really pretty awkward compared to this string of women he'd apparently dated in the past. At least she wasn't an idiot, which was a consolation. 'But, for me, marriage is more than liking someone. It's about *loving* them. Don't you see that? What you're describing might work at creating a marriage that doesn't hit the rocks, but, on the other hand, it would be a marriage without...that spark. It would be flat.' Though not for her, she thought, never for her, because she would be bringing to it all the love at her disposal and wouldn't that make it even harder to tolerate?

Bruno, for once, looked away and gave his head a little shake as if he was trying to clear it or else making his mind up about something.

'Isn't that some kind of start, though?' he asked roughly. 'I mean...you could learn to feel...to love me, couldn't you?'

The hesitation in his voice filled her with sudden, wild confusion. 'What are you getting at?'

'I am trying to tell you that…I don't see this marriage as one of convenience. It wouldn't be. At least, not for me.'

'I don't know what you're trying to say.'

'Aren't you women supposed to be intuitive?' Bruno asked in a voice that bordered on the plaintive. He shot her a frustrated look from under his ridiculously long lashes that made her want to smile.

'And isn't Bruno Giannella supposed to be fearless?' Katy asked.

'Supposedly,' he said with a reluctant smile. 'Except I'm a little scared right now because I love you and I want to marry you and I want to persuade you that even if you don't love me, you will. You can. You just need to give it time.'

A chorus of angels began singing in her head. Bruno loved her. Her mouth parted into a smile and then she was grinning like a fool.

'You just said that you loved me,' Katy breathed.

'I do. Love you. Adore you. Call it what you will.'

'But when?' She was hanging onto his every word and keen to prolong the confession that had sent her soaring up into the stratosphere.

'It crept up on me,' Bruno admitted. 'One minute I was wondering whether you would ever be able to perform the simplest of chores on the computer, the next minute I was watching out for you and making sure that I spent as much time as possible in your company.'

This was music to her ears. Katy sighed rapturously. 'All this time,' she murmured, 'loving you and thinking that you would never be able to feel the same way about me…'

Bruno stilled and then smiled. 'You would have walked away from our relationship when you loved me?' He caressed her face and pulled her tenderly towards him so that he could touch her gently parted lips with his own.

'It never occurred to me that you could actually love someone like me,' Katy broke apart to say unsteadily. Lord, now she wanted to cry.

'My handkerchief's ready and waiting,' Bruno told her, reading her expression and smiling at her with such love that the tears dried up.

'I just think what would have happened if Isobel hadn't done what she'd done, if she hadn't gone running to the press with some made-up story about us, if we hadn't been thrown into that engagement.' It was a sobering thought.

'Yes—fate works in mysterious ways.' Bruno leaned back against the door and pulled her against him, quite an awkward manoeuvre taking into account her calf-length dress.

'I should be angry with Isobel,' Katy said, raising her face to his. She was half lying with her back pressed to his torso, and she moaned softly as his hand swept beneath the length of dress, skimming up her legs and finally resting possessively between her legs. 'But I'm not, because I love you so much, Bruno.' He rubbed the place where his hand was and she felt herself moisten at the feel of his fingers against her underwear.

'My darling.'

'Perhaps we should…head back to the hotel?' She knew that he had booked somewhere in London. It was incredible to think that she had not given it a passing thought because she had reckoned that by the time the night was over, they would be too.

'Hmm. I'm not sure I can wait that long.' He slid his

hand beneath the thin cotton of her briefs and Katy closed her eyes and wriggled as he explored her. 'You needn't worry about Harry,' Bruno whispered. 'Can't hear a thing. You can be as vocal as you like…'

Katy surrendered to the velvety voice, shocked by the strength of her need to make love to him right here and right now. The blacked-out windows offered perfect privacy—not that there was any need for them. It was pitch-black outside. They were no longer in the city, though where they were heading she had no idea. Maybe Harry had taken his employer at his word and was whisking them off to Brighton.

Thank goodness it was a big car. His jacket and trousers joined her dress in the footwell, and when they were finally naked the touch of their bodies against one another was like a blaze of pure heat.

This time, there were no uncertainties gnawing at the back of her mind as they made urgent, if confined, love. He sat and she sat on him, loving the view it gave her of his mouth reaching to suckle her nipple as she leaned towards him and controlled her movements until he was as desperate as she was for fulfilment.

They came together, their bodies slick with excitement, and she sank against him, curling into him with a little sigh of contentment.

'You never answered,' Bruno teased huskily. 'Will you marry me and make me the happiest man on the face of the earth?'

'How could any girl refuse a proposal like that?' Katy murmured.

'You'll make a perfect wife,' Bruno murmured into her ear, 'and a perfect mother…'

At which point it suddenly struck Katy that there had

been no protection used. She sat up and looked down at him with an anxious expression.

'Bruno! I could be pregnant!'

'Let's hope so, my love.' He smiled wolfishly at her. 'And if you're not, well... ''tomorrow is another day''.'

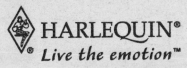

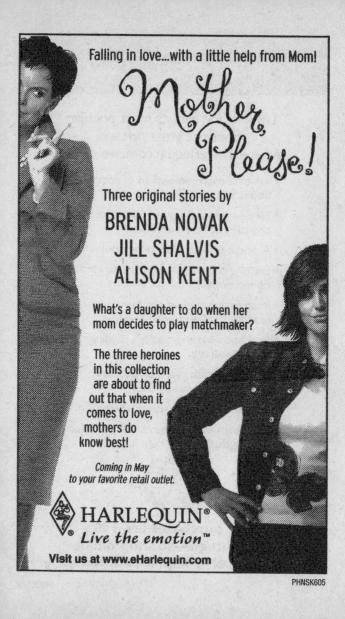

Coming Next Month

THE BEST HAS JUST GOTTEN BETTER!

#2391 THE OUTBACK MARRIAGE RANSOM Emma Darcy
At sixteen, Ric Donato wanted Lara Seymour—but they were worlds apart. Years later he's a city tycoon, and now he can have anything he wants.... Lara is living a glamorous life with another man, but Ric is determined to have her—and he'll do whatever it takes....

#2392 THE STEPHANIDES PREGNANCY Lynne Graham
Cristos Stephanides wanted Betsy Mitchell the moment he saw her, shy and prim in her chauffeur's outfit, at the wheel of his limousine.... However, the Greek tycoon hadn't bargained on being kidnapped—along with Betsy—and held captive on an Aegean island!

#2393 A SICILIAN HUSBAND Kate Walker
When Terrie Hayden met Gio Cardella she knew that there was something between them. Something that was worth risking everything for. But the proud Sicilian didn't want to take that risk. He had no idea what force kept dragging him back to her door....

#2394 THE DESERVING MISTRESS Carole Mortimer
May Calendar has spent her life looking after her sisters and running the family business—and she's determined not to let anyone take it away from her! Especially not arrogant tycoon Jude Marshall! But sexy, charming Jude is out to wine and dine her—how can she resist…?

#2395 THE MILLIONAIRE'S MARRIAGE DEMAND
Sandra Field
Julie Renshaw is shocked when Travis Strathern makes an outrageous demand: marriage! She is very attracted to him—but is she ready to marry for convenience? Travis always gets his own way—but Julie makes it clear that their marriage must be based on love as well as passion....

#2396 THE DESERT PRINCE'S MISTRESS Sharon Kendrick
Multimillionaire Darian Wildman made an instant decision about beautiful Lara Black—he had to have her! Their mutual attraction was scorching! Then Darian made a discovery that would change both their lives. He was the illegitimate heir to a desert kingdom—and a prince!